BOBCATS

by Matthew Weber

DEDICATION

Thanks to all my good buddies from the old days. You know who you are. This one's for you.

Prologue

Five sweaty seventh graders waited for the water fountain in the gymnasium lobby. Joey Kilgore tapped his foot at the end of the line, while each of the kids slurped their fill. Hot and winded from an intense game of dodgeball, he checked his watch. Not much time to spare. His tongue felt like dry leather, but he couldn't be tardy again to Mrs. Beckett's class. She'd hit the roof.

Two more kids from Phys Ed class crowded in behind him. The air grew stuffy with the sour smell of perspiration. Joey wiped his face with his shirttail. His turn at the fountain arrived, but Scotty Heckler shoved him aside and blocked him out like a basketball forward.

"Outta the way," Scotty grunted.

Joey teetered back but steadied his feet. "It was my turn!"

"Not anymore." Scotty bent over the fountain and drank.

Joey muttered, "Jackass," and instantly regretted it.

Scotty whirled around, water streaming from his chin like the drool of a mad dog. Sweat rolled down from his wavy brown hair across a minefield of acne. "What'd you say?"

Joey fumed and wanted to tell him to go gargle thumbtacks, but knew it would earn him a pounding. Scotty stood a head taller and had much bigger biceps.

"Nothing," Joey said.

"Yeah?" Scotty leaned in, just inches from his face. "That's what I thought."

Scotty's palms flew up and smacked Joey's ears like mallets. A dart-like sting pierced his eardrums. Joey clutched his head and staggered back into another student. All sound went faint and distant as though he'd fallen down a deep well.

Scotty smirked at him then disappeared in a blur. A rocket from the other side of the room had knocked him off his feet. Scotty and his attacker tumbled across the floor into a corner. The tackler leapt up first and shoved Scotty back down when he tried to stand.

Dancing on the balls of his feet with fists raised in a boxer's stance, Zack Traweek—"Trainwreck" to his friends—hopped around Scotty, ready to strike again if he didn't back off.

As the cotton in Joey's ears cleared away, the other kids spread into a semicircle to cheer and jeer the action.

"I told you before," Trainwreck said to Scotty, "don't mess with the Bobcats."

"Do we have a problem here?" Coach Horton's voice echoed from across the gym where he stood in the doorway of the locker room.

Trainwreck dropped his fists. Scotty stood up and brushed himself off.

Nobody answered, so Joey shouted through the open doorway, "No, Coach. No problem."

"Then get to class."

"Yes, sir."

The crowd dispersed.

As Scotty slinked away, he grumbled, "This ain't over…"

Joey and Trainwreck followed him at a distance toward the locker room.

"Thanks," Joey muttered through a pang of embarrassment. Trainwreck had swooped in to save the day. This made Joey the damsel in distress.

Trainwreck shrugged and smiled. "Just glad I can bring something to the troop."

Trainwreck was not a large guy. What he brought to the troop was courage.

And courage they would need.

Their troop was called the Bobcats.

This is their story.

Chapter 1 – Joey

"You'll be the man of the house now."

Joey placed the flowers at the foot of his father's headstone, the polished granite still shiny from the engraver. Thunder rippled in the distance as the sky to the south darkened.

As much as Joey loved his father, he resented him for having spoken those words from the hospital bed. *The man of the house…* The words were impossible to live up to. A boy should never lose his dad at such a young age, and it was unfair to have to shoulder that blow while also being tasked with such an impossible assignment.

Joey had always modeled his concept of a *man* after his father, who'd always been the family's provider, protector, repairman, and all-around superhero. Joey knew how to do none of those things.

The man of the house… The words echoed in his mind with the strange resonance he'd heard in the voice of a dream version of his father—an impostor who wore his dad's same warm smile but had black holes where his eyes should be.

Joey had once read about black holes, the dark, swirling voids that suck in all other forms of matter, much like the limitless responsibilities his dad had charged him with. A bottomless pit of expectations he could never fill.

"I hope I don't let you down, Dad."

He spruced up the flower bouquet his mom had asked him

to deliver, then stood up and hooked his backpack over a shoulder, wiping his eyes.

"You okay?" Davey Hopewell asked from the roadside, where he and Trainwreck waited on their bicycles. Davey wore his trademark blue and red Atlanta Braves baseball hat over neck-length black hair.

"Yeah, I'm fine." Joey cleared his throat. "Let's go."

He tore away from the gravesite, telling himself nothing could be gained by moping around. They had work to do. Important work. His father, Joseph Kilgore, had been founder of the Bobcats. Now, Joey and his friends had to carry on the legacy, and they were determined to complete the journey they'd all been planning for nearly a year, plans that had preceded his dad's diagnosis, and his swift decline. Since this Friday was a "teacher workday" that afforded the kids a three-day weekend, the Bobcats planned to hike The Gauntlet across Black Oak Mountain.

Joey threw his leg over his silver BMX. "Where's Paul and Clarence?"

"Meeting us at HQ," Trainwreck said.

Joey gave a nod and took off. The three Bobcats zoomed down the cemetery hill with Trainwreck tailing Joey on his turquoise '80s-era freestyle bike with axle pegs and mag wheels, while Davey soared along on his black Huffy. The road led to Grayson Drive where Joey hung a left. The other two followed.

The Bobcats largely made up the rules to their troop as they went, rules Joey's father had started with his own childhood friends when he was eleven years old. When Joey had grown old enough to show an interest in camping, his dad told him about the Bobcats, named after that fearsome but elusive regional critter, his dad's favorite animal. Joey and his friends took inspiration and formed their own troop with his dad's help. They dubbed it "Order of the Bobcats, Trapper Valley Original," proudly named after their small Alabama town.

His dad, who had worked as the city's Parks and Recreation Manager, had secured them use of the ballpark's equipment hut for official meetings every Tuesday night. But the boys decided they also needed a secret, kids-only hideout where they could meet after school or during the long days of summer break. After a little exploration, they settled on an old, abandoned house on Potters Lane.

They pedaled along the sidewalk as the day fell to dusk, then swooped onto the Potters offshoot, the noise of vehicles dying as they curved around a bank of magnolias. The April air smelled of pine and fresh rain. Webbed with cracks and crumbling at the edges, the quiet road wound through the woods where two shotgun buildings at the peak had sat windowless for years. The wood floors had rotted, the roofs sagged and leaked. However, the second house along the lane still had both its front and back door, which made it an excellent clubhouse.

Two bicycles leaned against a tree in the front yard. Joey laid his own on the grass beside them.

"Who goes there?" came a voice from the front stoop as the glare of a cell-phone flashlight hit Joey's eyes.

"Bobcats," he said.

"Jeez," said their friend Clarence as he lowered the beam. "We've been waiting on you guys a hundred years."

Clarence Barkley and Paul "Bubba" Drabowski sat on the front steps of HQ, rounding out the five current members of the Bobcats.

"We had to make a pit stop," Joey said.

"A Bobcat is punctual," Clarence told him.

"Yeah, right." Joey walked up the steps with Davey and Trainwreck right behind him.

They all exchanged the secret Bobcat handshake. It involved a slap of the palm, a backslap, a hook of the fingers which morph into a gun made from your pointer, drop the hammer (your thumb), pinch an invisible cigarette, bring it to your lips for a drag, then drop it to the ground and grind it with your shoe. It took a minute for everyone to perform.

They gathered around Joey on the porch as he slid his backpack off and dug out a notebook. Time to review their plans. He opened the spiral pad and unfolded a large topographical map he'd marked up with colored pencil. Clarence shined the light on the papers as Joey traced a red line with his finger.

"Okay, this is the route. A one-way trip. Thirty miles. We start here, at the trailhead on Shady Grove Road. It's blocked by a crossing bar and not accessible by car, but ATVs still buzz all over those trails every weekend, so the path should still be good and worn down. At least, at the beginning."

"Thirty miles," said Clarence, the heaviest of the bunch. "Man…sounds like a lot of hiking."

"It's been thirty miles as long as we've been talkin' about it," Trainwreck said as the twin sprigs of blond cowlick, ever-present atop his head, bobbed like antennae. "It ain't grown."

"I know," Clarence said, "but still."

"How'd we get stuck with the only non-athletic black guy in the whole school?" Trainwreck said.

"I've got a glandular problem, Zack," Clarence snapped. "And you sound like a racist hick."

"A Bobcat is physically fit," Trainwreck said. He loved to get a rise out of the others, especially Clarence.

"Y'all put a sock in it," Paul said. "This is important."

The others usually listened to him, especially since he'd started going by Paul instead of "Bubba," the nickname his parents had given him.

"Yeah," Joey said. "If we're gonna pull this off, we've got to plan it right. I don't want to hike out into the middle of the woods, miles away from civilization, then have everything go haywire."

The others clammed up.

"The trail through the forest takes us to a small lake," Joey continued. "Supposed to be an old strip pit. Dad said we've got to follow the edge of the water around to the other side. Supposed to be a steep hill there, and we're supposed to climb to the top. The path picks up again there."

"Will the trail be marked?" Paul asked.

"Haven't we been through all this?" Trainwreck asked.

"Don't know if it's marked," Joey said to Paul. "Dad said it used to be, but it's been years. The whole hike is a pretty straight shot, though. The lake is due east from the entrance. Then the path kind of winds to the top of the mountain and follows the ridgeline. We'll hit a few valleys on the way to Lonesome Bridge, and I'm sure we'll have to zigzag a bit, 'cause no telling how long it's been since somebody's hiked it. The trail ends near the Oak Hill soccer fields."

"You know it'll be all grown up," Clarence said. "It won't be easy to just blaze through the forest. I mean, you've got to factor in all the effects of climate change since your dad hiked the trail. Weeds like poison ivy surge in growth by like 150 percent in areas with high carbon dioxide."

Trainwreck looked at Clarence and rolled his eyes. "Jeez, you're a nerd. You scared, cupcake?"

"You wish."

"If it was easy, there'd be no point in doing it," Paul said. "It's called the *Gauntlet* for a reason. It's a challenge. A rite of passage."

"I know," Clarence said.

"It's what separates the men from the boys…and how we're gonna set ourselves apart from the other lame-Os in town," Joey said. "Our survival skills."

"I *know*," Clarence insisted. "I just want everybody to realize what we'll be dealing with."

"We'll be dealing with Mother Nature," Joey said.

"*I* sure ain't afraid of Mother Nature," Trainwreck piled on. "We'll be doing something nobody else in town has done for years. 'Cause nobody else has the cojones."

"It's supposed to rain."

"You don't have to go if you don't want, Clarence," Joey said.

Everybody stared at Clarence. He looked at his feet. "I'll go. If Mom and Dad will let me."

"And if they don't?" Trainwreck asked.

"Well. Maybe I'll go anyway."

Chapter 2 – Downtown Birmingham

Charles Daniel Nelson, known as "C.D." to friends and enemies alike, had never been summoned to Mr. Heidecker's office downtown, but a gun in his face changed that.

When the Lincoln came to a stop in the parking deck of a skyscraper, the large black man in the front seat moved his pistol in a way that told C.D. it was time to exit the back. C.D. did as instructed. The man with the gun slipped it into the pocket of his charcoal overcoat and stepped out along with the driver, an equally intimidating white guy sporting a pale shaved head and an ivory suit. They escorted C.D. to an elevator where Whitey shoved him on the shoulder as the doors parted. C.D. stepped inside. The other two followed.

The doors slid closed, and Blackie pressed the button for the 22nd level.

Top floor…how fancy, thought C.D. He wondered whether Mr. Heidecker would grant him a last meal, and if so, would he be allowed to order something fancy to match the setting.

Don't be so grim, he thought. *Maybe he'll just have these two assholes break my legs.*

They ascended silently, and once the elevator jolted to a stop, the doors opened with a whisper. Whitey nudged him through the doors of the elevator.

C.D. stepped onto a marble floor inside a lobby with ornately trimmed hardwood wall paneling and a massive mahogany desk with corbels at the corners. A smiling receptionist with a bob hairdo gave a curt nod to Blackie and said, "Mr. Heidecker is expecting you."

He swept past her, and C.D. followed so Whitey wouldn't shove him again.

Down a hallway to the left, they encountered two large double doors with elegant leaf patterns carved into the woodwork. Blackie knocked softly on the door, and a voice said something from the other side. He pressed the latch, opened it and entered, looking back to C.D. with a gesture to follow. Whitey pulled up the rear.

The dimly lit room maintained a similar décor; richly stained wood walls with elaborate molding detailed with layered beads, swoops and ogees that must have taken skilled craftsmen long hours to cut and shape by hand and tool.

Elevated on a hardwood platform beneath a large wall tapestry depicting a serpentine dragon, stood another grand desk, hexagonal in shape, which encircled a large-back leather chair turned toward a glass wall that overlooked the city lights of the Birmingham nightscape.

"You owe me money, Mr. Nelson," spoke a voice from the chair.

"Mr. Heidecker, look, I can explain."

"You owe me big."

"I swear, it wasn't my fault. I got robbed. Three dickheads in ski masks—"

"I don't care, Mr. Nelson."

"They took it all. The whole damn kilo first night I had it.

Had to be a setup. Broke into my place and—"

A hand shot up from the side of the chair, a small, wrinkled hand that pointed two fingers at the ceiling. C.D. took it as a sign to shut up, so he shut up.

"I don't care about your problems." Heidecker slowly turned his chair around. He wore an expensive-looking suit and a huge gold watch. With thinning black hair combed backed from his heavily lined face, he had a dark dime-sized mole in the center of his forehead—a third eye, which C.D. found difficult not to stare at. "I only care about *my* problems."

"Yes, sir."

"And right now, my problem is an unpaid debt. You were fronted merchandise by Vinnie the Cat. It was my merchandise. You claim to no longer have it, and you now owe Vinnie money for the merchandise. When you owe money to Vinnie the Cat, you owe me. Do you understand?"

"I can round up the money, I swear."

"If you could round up the money, then why haven't you done so?"

"I'm sorry. I really am. But twenty-five grand is a hell of an unforeseen expense."

"I'm sure you're aware of how I handle people who do not pay what they owe me."

"I will absolutely pay you what I owe. I swear to Christ."

"Oh, I know that," Heidecker said, his jaw jutting out slightly from his pockmarked chin. "And you'll pay with interest."

"Yes, sir. Whatever you say."

"What I say is that you're out of time. Your debt is due, yet you claim to have an inability to pay. Therefore, you must buy yourself more time."

"Please. Just a little more time for me to figure something out. I've got a lead on a job. I only need to work out the angles."

"There's only one thing I'm offering that will buy you time. I need a driver."

"Yes, sir. Okay. I can do that."

"You'll have a partner."

"Okay."

"You'll be driving for the Cleaver."

As those words crawled into his ears, C.D. looked down at his hands and folded them together. The breath left his lungs in a sigh. The prospect of two broken legs didn't seem so bad now.

"The Cleaver?"

Heidecker gave an almost imperceptible nod. "He doesn't care to drive. Should be a fairly simple task for you. He does all the dirty work. You just need to help with transportation and disposal."

"But, sir—"

"I know, I know. Nobody wants to work with the Cleaver," Heidecker said. He picked up an unlit cigar from an ashtray, examining it between his fingertips. "What kind of vehicle do you drive, Mr. Nelson?"

"What? I, uh…I drive a Mustang."

"A Mustang. Fine," Heidecker said. "Do you know what Mr.

Malone drives? The African-American gentleman behind you?"

"I don't know. A Lincoln?"

Heidecker shook his head. "No. Mr. Jacks drives the Lincoln. Mr. Malone drives a huge pickup truck with monstrously sized wheels. I always thought that was interesting because I associate such vehicles with rural white men, the type who wear cowboy hats and go to rodeos. The type who drive big trucks they don't need just for the show of it, as if to compensate for something they lack. Maybe a small intellect. Or a small penis." He looked over C.D.'s shoulder. "But you're a smart guy, Mr. Malone, and you don't have a small penis. Do you?"

"It's huge," Mr. Malone said.

Heidecker stared at C.D. "Would you like to see Mr. Malone's penis to verify its size, Mr. Nelson?"

"No, sir. I would not."

"Good answer. We'll take Mr. Malone's word for it. About the truck… Last week we had a problem with a fellow who'd been caught stealing from us. Remember that, Mr. Jacks?"

"I do."

The next question was directed at C.D. "Do you know how we handled the thief?"

"No, sir," he answered.

"These two fine fellows handled him using Mr. Malone's pickup truck." Mr. Heidecker dropped the cigar into the ashtray and stared at C.D. intently with all three eyes. "You see, first they tied him up. Then, Mr. Jacks held him down while Mr. Malone backed one of those big wheels right over his head. *Crunch!* A hell of mess; wasn't it, Mr. Jacks?"

"Like a crushed melon, sir."

"And so…" Heidecker said with an air of finality, "you either agree, right here and now, to drive the Cleaver on a particularly nasty errand I need him to oversee. Or else Jacks and Malone will flatten your skull beneath a big black truck tire."

C.D. swallowed a thick gulp of air. "Looks like I'll be driving then."

Heidecker laced his fingers and nodded. "Yes, it looks like you'll be driving. I'm told the man stays on Black Oak Mountain. We'll get you a map."

Chapter 3 – Trainwreck

Trainwreck clamored through the screen door of the two-bedroom farmhouse where he lived with his grandparents. He'd been fleeing two stray dogs that had been terrorizing him on his walk home from school the last several days. The next time he left the house, he planned to carry a baseball bat. He hated the idea of hurting an animal, but if those dogs didn't lay off, he'd have to get mean.

"Howdy, Gramma," Trainwreck greeted while catching his breath.

He dropped his backpack and ear buds onto the couch where she sat.

"Have a good day, hon?" she asked absently, immersed in a crossword puzzle.

"Was okay. Gramps home?"

Staring at the empty squares, she mouthed words to herself in silent concentration.

"Is Gramps home?" he asked louder.

"What? Oh. No, he's out in his truck somewhere. You know how he is. Always busy doing nothing."

Only two days before the trip, Train was hoping his grandfather would have some old hiking gear he could borrow. Maybe a canteen and a flashlight. He plopped down on the couch next to his grandmother and kicked off his sneakers. "Me and the guys are going camping this weekend. Out in the woods."

"Camping?"

"Yeah. Roughing it."

She tugged an Afghan blanket higher on her lap, but her eyes never left the paper booklet. The pages were filled with puzzles, and she'd finish one right after another. "You don't think you'll get scared out in those woods?"

"Scared? Heck naw, Gramma. I'm thirteen years old, I ain't scared."

"If you say so." Finally, she turned to him. "Ain't it supposed to rain cats and dogs?"

"I don't know. Maybe. I don't reckon I'll melt."

She returned her attention to the crossword. "Might catch a cold."

"I'm too fast to catch," he said.

Peering up from her puzzle, she raised an eyebrow. He grinned in return.

"Well, don't leave your shoes there on the floor," she said. "Sounds like you'll need 'em, Jesse Owens."

"Jesse who?"

Once again, Gramma returned to the crossword and didn't bother to answer.

Trainwreck grabbed his sneakers and climbed the stairs to his bedroom. His father was serving ten years for armed robbery, and his mother lived two counties away "sorting herself out," as his Grandma would say. His grandparents had raised him, and as long as nobody phoned them with a complaint, they didn't much care how he spent his time. This gave him a lot of freedom. In the eyes of the other Bobcats, that freedom meant Trainwreck had it easy, but he didn't always see it that way.

From beneath his bed, he pulled out the Patagonia backpack Gramma had bought at a yard sale and began to fill it with crucial items for the trip. Clean drawers. Two t-shirts and a comb for his cowlicks. He packed a cigarette lighter, a bundle of rope, and spare sneakers. Some M&Ms, half a pouch of beef jerky, a can of Skoal tobacco he'd nabbed from Gramps, and his trusty MP3 player because he loved classic rock. Most importantly, he packed the camouflage-handled survival knife his father had given him before being sentenced.

Trainwreck unscrewed the compass that capped its end and peered into the hollow handle. The plastic casing contained fishing line, two hooks, lead weights, plastic-wrapped matches, and a wire saw for cutting tree branches—everything a guy might need to survive whatever challenge Mother Nature threw at him. Satisfied with his supplies, he screwed the compass back on, slid the blade into its faux-leather sheathe, and packed it in the bag. To Trainwreck, that knife was Excalibur.

Chapter 4 – Nerves

C.D. gripped the wheel of the Ford Expedition like he helmed an armored tank. He'd boosted the ride in Walker County, hoping the hayseed sheriff would be too preoccupied with the meth-heads to make the theft a priority. The big vehicle gave him the height to look down at other motorists as he was meant to see the world, but being partial to flashy sports cars like his own Shelby Mustang, he worried the giant SUV made him look like a kid in an oversized suit. Still, a smaller car would not work. From what he'd heard, the Cleaver was a titan, more than seven feet tall and stacked like three-course brick. The last thing he wanted to suggest to a mountain-sized contract killer was that he cram himself into a tiny seat for the duration of their trip. *Don't prod the monster*—that seemed like a good policy for C.D. to maintain his health and safety.

And safety was a grave concern. This job was nowhere near as simple as it sounded. Driving the Cleaver meant *surviving* the Cleaver, a name he'd always considered more myth than man. A man that he never imagined he would meet face to face. A walking legend said to have black blood, ice for a heart, and a history of killing the very partners who were assigned to him for nothing more than giving him a funny look.

That sleazeball, Vinnie the Cat… This was all his fault. With his pointy chin and batwing hairdo, only Vinnie had known when and where C.D. had the coke on him. He'd hired three thugs in ski masks and organized the heist of his own drugs, knowing he was too valuable to Heidecker's enterprise to catch heat as long as he could finger a handy culprit. C.D. had no hard proof of it, but his gut told him Vinnie had sold him out, and his gut was all he needed. As soon as he got on the sunny side of this driving assignment, he planned to make things square with Vinnie, one way or the other.

After two hours on the freeway, C.D. took a non-descript exit that had no traffic light, gas station, or any other notable landmark aside from its DOT mile marker. Following his GPS coordinates, he veered to the right and followed a sleepy four-lane for nine miles to his next turn, a winding two-lane county route that skirted the foot of a mountain into a thickening forest. The road grew ragged and narrow, and the trees closed in, branching overhead with a greedy reach that obscured the sun. C.D.'s nerves tingled and stirred. He shifted in his seat, unable to get comfortable, scratching at himself as though ants milled around beneath his skin.

Who the hell lives in the woods, deep in the middle of nowhere?

The answer was obvious. *A monster lives here.*

He shuddered and pulled out a pack of Marlboros, tapping one out and pinching the filter with his lips. He lit it, inhaled, blew smoke out the window, and felt just a little bit better.

Paul Drabowski handed his stepdad the Busch tallboy he'd wanted from the fridge. "I'll be camping in the woods for a couple days."

"Camping? Hell, Bubba. Why you wanna do something like that?" Donnie didn't look at him when he spoke, sunken into a recliner with his eyes glued to a pro wrestling match. He took a swig, and a trickle of beer ran down his stubbly chin and dripped onto his undershirt.

"It's Paul, not 'Bubba.' I'm going with friends. Hiking the Gauntlet. Joey's dad was supposed to take us before he died. Same trip he took with his friends when he was our age. It's a big deal to Joey, so I told him he could count me in."

"Hiking the what? Ain't it supposed to rain?"

"I'll bring a poncho."

"Break his neck!" Donnie shouted at the screen. "Kill him!"

"We're leaving in the morning. Should be back Sunday night."

"Your mom said it's okay?"

His mother worked nights as a nurse at the hospital. She'd told him over the phone to ask Donnie's permission.

"She just said to let you know where I'd be."

Paul's true father, Jonathon Paul Drabowski, had died honorably serving his country in the Middle East when Paul was a toddler. Paul barely remembered his dad's face, but revered the man and his sacrifice, especially when compared to Donnie.

Donnie took a pull from his beer. He kept his hair long and shaggy, and never tucked in his shirttail, which is why Paul kept his own hair trimmed high and tight and always maintained a neat appearance. Paul had never understood the appeal his mom found in the lout, so he made a point to serve as a stark comparison and a model of the type of man she deserved—more like his dad.

"Yeah, yeah, just stay out of the hospital," Donnie told him. "And keep your nose clean. You get yourself in trouble with the law, don't be calling me. No money for bail."

"I won't." Paul had never been in trouble with the law. His stepfather, on the other hand…

"Pick up the chair!" Donnie said. "Hit him with the chair!"

Paul left the den and went to his bedroom to pack.

In an aluminum-framed backpack he'd borrowed from his cousin, Paul stuffed a change of clothes, a poncho, pocketknife, compass, binoculars, granola bars, a flashlight with extra batteries, and a copy of *To Kill a Mockingbird* for his assigned summer reading. At the bottom of the frame, he bungie-corded a rolled pup tent along with his sleeping bag. And he couldn't leave without the framed 3x5 photograph of his smiling girlfriend, Candace Worton, which was propped on the nightstand. Paul kissed her face before sliding Candace inside the pack.

Chapter 6 – The Pickup

C.D. brought the Expedition to a stop and shifted into park. After winding down miles of broken backcountry asphalt, he'd finally happened upon the crumbling civil war-era graveyard that marked his turn down a long, desolate dirt path. He let the engine idle in front of what could only be the home of the fabled man of the hour, for no sane person would inhabit this godforsaken shithole hidden in a clearing within the thick forest walls.

A sane person might have installed a sidewalk or decorated the place with shrubbery, maybe planted a flowerbed or stuck some crappy pink flamingos in the ground. But here, the ghastly shapes that hung from the trees or stood wired to tall posts looked like the forgotten runes of an ancient pagan tribe. Metal and bones, branches and vines, welded and sculpted into ten-foot scarecrows and swooping winged beasts. Among a junkyard of corroded farm implements and bundles of bailing wire, dark, hulking humanoids posed with groping claws and antlered heads. Flanking the yard were slender sentries towering with rusty iron skeletons, hoop-steel ribs and dried kudzu capes. Man-sized spiders crafted with bent rebar legs and railroad-spike fangs creeped over the lawn and peered from behind trees. As he studied the macabre statuary, C.D. had a nagging impulse to throw the Ford in reverse and drive like hell. Staying here simply could not end well.

But to leave would seal his fate. He could only run so far. Mr. Heidecker was known for his uncanny ability to reach a man anywhere. Forget Jacks and Malone, if C.D. were to split, Heidecker would send the Cleaver after him. That was a guarantee.

He lit another cigarette and stared at the house, which showed no sign of electricity or plumbing. Built of cinderblock and moldering wood, the Cleaver's home was a sparse, squarish structure with mortared walls and a patched, corrugated metal roof. A scattering of flat creek-bed stone lay around the perimeter as a rudimentary patio, and near the dented steel front door the carcasses of three skinless animals hung drying from the eaves. Flies buzzed around the meat, chickens pecked the dirt beneath them, and a few goats searched for weeds at the edge of the plot.

"Shit," C.D. muttered.

The choice of whether to bring his gun with him was a tricky one. He'd rarely felt more threatened in his life, but if the man who lived here saw him packing, he might shoot first and ask questions later.

"*Shit,*" he said again, then pulled his revolver from its holster and slid it beneath the seat. It had always been mostly for show, anyway.

Sitting behind that steering wheel, C.D. dreaded every ticking second. He took a deep breath and opened the door. He climbed out, flicked away his cigarette and walked with feigned confidence toward the house. His every instinct told him he was being watched. There would be no need to knock.

He took Heidecker's letter from the pocket of his sports coat, unfolded it, and held it high so whoever was watching could see it clearly.

"I was sent by Mr. Heidecker," he announced. "This is his letter. I'm supposed to pick up the Cleaver. I'm the driver."

A faint whisper passed C.D.'s ear. The paper twitched in his hand as a speeding arrow speared through it and plunked into a nearby tree trunk. His heart stopped for the duration of five beats—C.D. was sure of it. The arrow had missed his skull by mere inches.

He peered over his body to make sure it all remained intact and then released a frozen breath. He thought, *Jesus Christ! Was that necessary?* but dared not speak aloud. Too petrified to move, he stood there scanning the house but saw no one in the windows.

After a small eternity, the steel door of the house opened and out stepped the biggest, grizzliest creature C.D. had ever seen outside a zoo.

Clutching a crossbow, the man was a monster indeed; a mountain of muscle and hair emerged from the doorway and stood obscuring the entrance behind him. Like some fur-covered sasquatch, a gray beard caped his chest along with a colorless mane which draped over his protruding brow and colossal shoulders. Standing not just tall and broad but enormous in scope, he looked like something from a dark fable.

From somewhere in that tangled pelt, the man stared at C.D.

through shadowed eyes, studying him and weighing judgment.

C.D. swallowed, but his throat felt lined with sand. Again, he raised Heidecker's paper like some magical totem that might grant him immunity from being sentenced to death.

The beast that was the Cleaver huffed once and ducked back inside the murk of his house, closing the door firmly behind him.

C.D. waited for him. Patiently. For a very long time.

"So, can I go? I'll be back Sunday before bedtime," Davey Hopewell told his mother, who stirred a sizzling skillet of chicken and sautéed peppers. She'd been stewing on his request to go camping for the last two hours.

"Say no, say no!" teased his little sister Ana who stood at his mother's side.

"Anyone ever tell you that you're annoying?" he said to Ana.

Ana stuck out her tongue.

His mother pursed her lips. "You say Joey's mother will be home while you're camping?"

Davey nodded.

"And you'll go inside if you hear any thunder?"

"Of course." He felt rotten about the lie. He had told her they'd be camping in the Kilgores' back yard, because she would never have let him hike the mountain without adult supervision. Since he really would be camping, he figured he'd told only half a lie, which he hoped qualified as only half a sin.

His mom sighed and finally relented. "Just be careful, por favor?"

Davey's heart swelled. He reached for his mom who brightened and smiled as he gave her a tight hug and kissed her cheek. "I will! I'll be with the Bobcats. What could go wrong?"

With that, he dashed to his room at the other end of their

mobile home to gather his gear for the trip.

Adventure! Davey would have an honest-to-goodness adventure! Fascinated with nature and wildlife, he always preferred the outdoors to being cooped up inside, stuck in front of a TV or tablet. But his protective mother enforced a firm six o'clock curfew, which put strict limits on his quest for adventure. Now, with two whole nights and three days to face the elements with the other Bobcats, he'd have a chance to prove to himself, and to the others, what he was made of.

He'd been preparing for this moment for thirteen long years.

For Christmas, his parents had given him a military-style tactical outdoor backpack, and this would be its maiden voyage. At its bottom, he lashed his pup tent and sleeping bag. The outer pockets held a compass, first-aid kit, two maps, three pencils, binoculars, bug repellent, bear spray, a digital camera, and a Swiss Army knife. Inside the main pouch, he stuffed a plastic tarp, his folded clothes, spare sneakers, some peanuts, snack cakes, and most importantly, the white binder full of unorganized documents that comprised the official Bobcat handbook—its cover roaring with Davey's black Sharpie sketch of the fearsome feline. That three-ring binder held Davey's own notes and photographs, as well as pages ripped out of nature magazines, the *Boy Scout Handbook*, *The Dangerous Book for Boys*, and any number of books on hunting, fishing, or outdoor survival.

The making of the handbook, an ever-evolving work in progress, was a big deal among the Bobcats, and Davey was proud to have been entrusted with such a critical duty. He'd never had much influence on the world around him, but now he had a chance to establish an instructive tome with his friends that would shape the knowledge and build the character of all Bobcats to follow, maybe for generations to come. Davey wasn't about to screw it up.

He'd been granted this honor because the other guys trusted his innate ability to commune with nature and navigate the wilderness. These assumptions were based on their belief in his Native American heritage. The truth was that Davey's mother was half Mexican and his father Italian-American. He'd never bothered to correct his friends of their racial mistake, because the quiet awe they held for the American Indian, the naive but respectful view they held of that culture as characteristically noble and somehow mystical—traits they in turn attributed to *him*—made Davey feel special in a world where he didn't otherwise feel very special. So, if the Bobcats thought he was the man who should make the handbook, then he planned to make the best dang handbook they'd ever see.

Before wrapping it in plastic and stuffing it into his pack, he held the book at eye level and blew dust off the top as though it were an ancient and sacred artifact…which one day it just might be.

#

Startled by a noise after a long stretch of drowsy silence, C.D.

sat up behind the wheel of the Ford to see the Cleaver step out of his house's dark interior wearing a filthy, faded black overalls. The man dropped an oversize army duffel onto the ground, which landed with a heavy clang. Strange metal implements protruded from the open end of the canvas bag. Slamming the door behind him, the Cleaver hooked a massive padlock through the latch and clamped it shut between both hands. He hoisted up the green bag and pitched it onto his shoulder, bracing it against his side as he stalked toward the car on legs the size of oil drums.

Without a word, C.D. reached down and pressed a button along the floorboard that released the hatch. It floated open for the Cleaver, who rounded the far side of the vehicle. He shoved his equipment into the trunk, where it fell with a crash. He then approached the passenger door, opened it and looked over the interior, then climbed inside. The shocks moaned, and the Expedition tilted toward the Cleaver's side as he settled into the seat.

C.D. fumbled his keychain around the ignition. Finally, the right key slid in, and he started the engine. Throwing the Ford into reverse, he sped away from the place with a demon at his side.

#

"A real shame about that boy's father," Juanita Barkley said to Clarence from across the dinner table.

"That's the whole point of the sleepover, Mom," Clarence

said. "Mr. K. was supposed to take us camping this weekend. Since he can't, we thought we'd do the next best thing and stay the weekend together at Joey's place."

Clarence tucked another forkful of chicken stir-fry into his mouth and looked at his plate, so his mother couldn't see his lying eyes.

"A sleepover for two nights?" his mother pried. "You sure Mrs. Kilgore is willing to put up with a houseful of smelly boys for that long?"

"Bobcats smell good, Mom. Besides, we'll be staying in a tent. And yes, she's okay with it. It was her idea." He was really laying it on thick and knew that one simple phone call from his mother to Mrs. K. would reveal his deception and seal his fate for an eternity. His entire future hinged on that not happening.

His mother chewed silently for a while, and to Clarence the suspense was like medieval torture.

"I'll be back home before dark on Sunday," he said.

"What do y'all have planned? Better not be any guns involved."

"No, Mom, nothing like that."

"Or cigarettes. Or booze. Or women!"

"Mom, please..." he said.

She giggled, teasing him, and took a sip of tea. "I'll speak to your father about it."

"When?"

"When he gets home."

"When will that be?"

"I'm not sure. He had three surgeries scheduled for today, and you know how that goes. Surgeons are in high demand. That's why you should follow in his footsteps."

"I know, I know…" Clarence sighed and took another bite of teriyaki chicken. It could be hours before his dad got home.

The suspense was killing him.

Chapter 8 – The Gathering

Spiders. Snakes. Wolves. Wild boars…. Do bears roam the mountain too?

As Janice Kilgore carried two trays piled with breakfast across the lobby of the Burger Hut, she mentally chronicled the many threats her son Joey might face in the wilderness. Insect bites. Allergic reactions. Broken bones or serious illness. The thoughts turned her stomach.

The morning of the hike had arrived, and Mrs. Kilgore insisted the boys meet at her house so she could treat them to a hearty meal before their journey. She loaded everyone into her Cherokee and hauled them to their favorite local eatery, where they shoveled down eggs, bacon, and biscuits with white gravy. It was a small something she could do before there would be *nothing* she could do, entrusting her son's safety to his own judgement and that of his friends, somewhere deep in the forest.

The idea of the boys hiking without Joey's father turned her stomach. She couldn't handle losing Joey, not after losing her husband. She acknowledged this as a selfish thought, but damn it, it was an honest one. Watching Joey wolf down his biscuit felt like attending his final meal. It bound Janice's insides into a tangled knot. Her sister out in California thought she'd gone nuts by allowing the trip to go forward, but how could she say no? They had all been planning it for so long, and to clip their wings now would mean they'd soon have their noses to a video screen like all the other little zombies of the modern era—exactly what Joseph had been working against. So, she would keep the waterworks dammed for the moment. At least until the boys were out of sight. Then she'd let herself go to pieces.

"Clarence, your cell phone is completely charged up?" she asked him. He was the only Bobcat with a mobile.

"Yes, ma'am," he answered.

"Good. Now let's go over this one more time." She stood over the boys to review yet again the checklist of emergency items she'd urged the troop to pack. For the first time that morning, the Bobcats grumbled as she began calling out the items—*spare shoes, dried food, canteen,* etc. On hearing their groan, she surrendered with a sigh and folded the list closed.

"I'm sorry," she told Joey, as she slumped into her seat.

He wiped gravy from his lip. "Mom, it's okay. If you didn't worry, you wouldn't be a good mother. We'll be fine. I promise. Dad taught us well. It's just a little camping trip. We won't even be far out of town."

"I know, but the rain…"

"Rain is just water, Mom. We're *made* out of water, like sixty percent. Clarence told me that."

Janice looked at the other boys. Clarence, his cheeks bulging with eggs, took a fork from his mouth and nodded emphatically.

"I'm worried about the forty percent that's *not* made of water," she said.

Joey stood up, leaned over and kissed her forehead. "Love you, Mom. Don't worry." He wiped her forehead with a napkin. "Sorry, you had some gravy."

The boys laughed at that, but Janice couldn't quite do the same.

Their drive to the mouth of the Gauntlet felt to her like a trip to the gallows. While the boys laughed and cut up in the back seats, she noticed the darkening sky and tingled with dreadful intuition.

Janice dropped the boys at the trailhead. She hugged Joey and kissed his cheek. Her heart quivered as the boys hiked away. When they finally disappeared into the woods, she clasped her face and let it all out.

#

"Mind if I smoke?" These were the first words C.D. had dared to utter during the drive.

The Cleaver had not spoken or so much as acknowledged his presence. The big beast of a man sat perfectly still with his arms crossed in stony silence, facing the windshield. His mane of hair hung so low over his brow that C.D. could not see his eyes, nor did he want to. Was the man asleep?

C.D. somehow knew he wasn't asleep, because sleep would present a moment of vulnerability, and vulnerability belied everything he knew of the man.

To settle his nerves, C.D. tapped a cigarette out of the pack, lit up, and inhaled with gusto. He lowered the window four inches to expel the cloud of smoke, cutting a glance at the passenger to gauge his reaction.

There was none. Only silence and stench.

The Cleaver smelled awful. He stunk of old sweat, sewage, and rotting flesh. It was nearly overwhelming, and C.D. had fought the urge to gag for the first few miles of the drive. The cigarette helped. C.D. imagined the Cleaver must slaughter his own food, cook over a fire pit, and shit in the woods. Living alone in a jungle—why bathe? The filth that covered the man must contain parasites and disease.

C.D. inched closer to his door and rubbed away an itchy feeling on his arms. He eyeballed the GPS readout on the dashboard. They were assigned to an address in a high-end suburb of Birmingham, an area familiar to C.D. from a few burglary jobs he'd pulled some years ago. Hillbrook Heights was populated with the million-dollar homes of pasty, country-club assholes. Considering the nasty business they had ahead of them, if the mark lived at that address, then they probably deserved what they had coming. Some dickhead named Goldstein had pissed off the wrong people.

"So, the job we're heading to," C.D. asked before he thought better of it. "What'd this Goldstein guy do to deserve a visit from the Cleaver?"

He got no answer. The Cleaver merely sat there statuesque, looming like a dark cloud.

C.D. returned his attention to the cigarette, which made for better company.

Chapter 9 – The Gauntlet

For Joey, the journey didn't really begin until his mom was well out of sight. The Bobcats climbed the hill that broke away from the road and followed an ATV path that zigzagged into the woods, where a leafy canopy of towering trees folded them into its clutches. They crested the shady incline, and the well-worn path twisted through a steep V-groove into a tall rock formation. Behind them, the faint sounds of passing vehicles faded away. The new calm accentuated the crunch of twig and branch underfoot, the rustle of dry leaves, and the lively chirping of singing birds. And that's when Joey felt it.

He felt a wildness within him—a sense of abandon and peril, the nervous tingle of endless possibilities, knowing anything might happen out here. Good or bad, wrought of Heaven or Hell. He was spreading newly formed wings for his very first flight. They were now on their own to live their dreams in a natural sense, unbound by civilization, technology, rules or parents…

Joey took it in with a robust breath and found the freedom exhilarating, and a tiny bit terrifying, knowing that with dreams lurked nightmares, like trolls hiding beneath bridges, trolls with black-hole eyes who might eat kids his age. And bridges were easy to spot, but anything could lurk out here in the forest. Anywhere.

People told campfire stories about this mountain.

He smiled at the prickle of fright stirring within himself, soaking up the sensation. This was living, facing the world unshielded. No journeys were ever ventured by watching through a window. One had to participate, had to engage the elements, endure the rain and wind on their face, skin their knees and taste the dirt to know their heart was truly beating. For Joey, this hike was a taste of something wonderful.

He led the troop around the thick, gray trunk of a huge maple, where the path resumed a sharp leftward swoop through the undergrowth. They hiked a ways before the path opened to a lake, which came sooner than Joey had expected. On the shore lay a scattering of empty beer cans and a discarded pair of panties, which Trainwreck stuck onto the end of a stick to make himself a flag. Following their map, they wound around the trail along the bank.

"I can't believe we're really doing this," Joey said. "Finally hiking the Gauntlet. This is awesome."

"*I feel good, danna-nanna-nanna-na!*" Trainwreck gave his best James Brown impression.

"I'm serious. I feel like an explorer or something. Like a pioneer from the Old World, or some hero from a book."

"You too?" Davey said from the middle of the line. He had a habit of phrasing everything as a question. "Like Indiana Jones, right?"

"Like Columbus," said Trainwreck.

"Like an epic hero," Paul added. "Like Odysseus."

"Yeah," Joey said. "Like that. You feel like that, Clarence?"

"Sure," Clarence huffed from the back of the pack as he

leaned against a broken tree branch that he'd been using as a walking stick. "It's an adventure. We've got to be careful out here, though. The woods can be dangerous."

"Extremely dangerous," Trainwreck said. "We might get torn to pieces by a rabid squirrel."

The Bobcats chuckled, except for Clarence. "I'm just sayin'… I know you've heard the stories about what goes on in the hills out here, away from the neighborhoods."

"I'll tell you what happens around here," Trainwreck said. "A bunch of nothin'. Trapper Valley is Dullsville."

"You don't buy that, do you?" Davey asked Trainwreck. "They only want us to *think* this place is dull. For our own protection. Everybody knows the adults cover up all the weirdness that happens."

Trapper Valley was a beehive of superstitious gossip and eerie lore. At the ripe age of thirteen, Joey, like Trainwreck, found the tales hard to believe. Especially given the glaring lack of evidence which he'd long hoped to find. Growing up, they'd heard all the stories of Bigfoot, monster fish, vengeful ghosts, crazed killers, and forest witches. These made for enjoyable campfire tales, but with age came the disillusionment of reality. It wasn't that Joey didn't want to believe—he very much did— but at his age, a lot of kids began to chalk up the stories to the imaginations of other local kids who'd come before them. Kids who found the town so boring that they created fantasies as a diversion from the bland reality of living in a place where nothing much happened.

"I'm not saying I believe everything I hear," Clarence said. "I'm just telling you that weird things happen around these parts. Bad things that grownups don't tell us. They whisper about them after we're in bed."

"Y'all don't believe the stories?" Davey said.

"My mom…she thinks the woods around here are cursed," Clarence continued. "She says this mountain attracts evil like moths to a candle. I had to tell her I was staying the weekend at Joey's, because she'd throw a fit if she knew I was out here."

"For real," Davey added. "My mother told me about a family who were camping here on the mountain. They say one night a demon with huge claws tore into their tent. It was as big as a bear but all gray and hairless. It snatched up their baby and ran off into the woods. You think I'd be here now, if she knew where I was?"

The troop followed Joey along the narrowing path, which succumbed to tangled vines, piled leaves, and downed branches, slowing their pace as they stomped through the brush.

"Cursed…" Trainwreck grumbled. "Hogwash." Being raised by his elderly grandparents had given him a penchant for using their cornpone expressions, which often made the others giggle, as they did on hearing this one. "Ain't no monsters out here to worry about. Besides, no monster better mess with us…Bobcats bite back."

Joey cast a look back at his friends and saw Clarence shrug.

"Maybe it's not monsters we've got to worry about." Clarence said. "I read that bobcats as a species are natural born survivors, except for human interference. Man is their principal threat."

"Man?" Trainwreck said. "Well, I reckon that evens the score, seeing as we got five men here in our troop. I feel like that's some pretty good odds."

"We're not men, we're kids," Joey said.

"Speak for yourself," Trainwreck said. "Besides, if anything out here gives us any trouble—man or monster—I got a nasty surprise for 'em."

He elbowed past Joey to the head of the pack and turned to face the others, dropping his bag from his shoulder. The others gathered around as he worked down the zipper. He stuck his hand inside and fished around. What he pulled from the backpack made Clarence gasp and take a step backward.

Trainwreck laid the pistol in the palm of his left hand. He kept the barrel safely pointed away from everyone just as Joey's dad had instructed them and presented it to the circle of Bobcats as if it were a rare scientific specimen.

"Holy smokes," Joey said.

"Where'd you get that?" Davey asked.

"It's Gramps' gun," Trainwreck said. "It's a .45 caliber Smith & Wesson. He doesn't know I borrowed it."

"Nope," Clarence said while shaking his head. "No way. You can count me out. Either the gun goes, or I do."

The others looked at him.

"I'm serious. Nobody said anything about guns. Y'all know

how I feel about them. I don't want that anywhere near me."

"Clarence," Trainwreck said. "Don't let your parents brainwash you."

Mrs. Barkley, the type who would complain to every restaurant manager about every meal she'd ever ordered, also liked to organize protests or boycotts for political causes. Gun control was an issue forever fashionable, and she'd thrown an absolute tantrum the time Joey's dad had organized a day at the local firing range to give the Bobcats instruction on firearm safety. Clarence had been strictly forbidden from attending, and afterward had to beg his mom to let him remain a member of the troop.

The other guys thought she was bonkers for making such a fuss.

"Nobody's brainwashing me," Clarence said. "Y'all don't even know how to use that thing. Don't you know there's like 17,000 firearm accidents a year in the U.S.? That's from dummies like us playing with guns we don't know how to use. Do you even have bullets for that thing?"

Trainwreck released the magazine then slid it back in the grip with a click. "Locked and loaded."

"Naw, forget this," Clarence said. "The gun's gotta go."

"I'd rather have it and not need it than need it and not have it," Trainwreck quoted a popular bumper sticker seen around town.

For Joey, the sight of the pistol was a fitting omen for what he anticipated of the trip, eliciting a tinge of both excitement and dread. Having a gun at the ready gave him an uneasy sense of security. There was no denying that anytime he had held one and squeezed off a round, he felt a surge of power. Whether that power was real or imagined, the *feeling* was real and it was nice. But power could be dangerous. Sure, a gun would come in handy if facing a bear, but the Bobcats were a clumsy lot and more apt to shoot off one of their own feet. In the end, he figured both Clarence and Trainwreck had excellent points. Why risk an accident if you don't need the gun? Why leave the gun if there's a risk that you'll need it?

Clarence, after waiting on his stone-faced friends and getting no response, dropped his head and shook it. "If that's the way it's going to be…" He turned and hiked back in the direction they had come.

"Look, I'll keep it hidden in my pack," Trainwreck called after him.

Clarence kept hiking away.

The other guys exchanged a look. Trainwreck, most begrudging of the decision, rolled his eyes and sighed. "Fine! Don't get your panties in a wad. I'll leave it here."

Clarence stopped. He turned back around. "You will?"

Trainwreck looked at the pistol and muttered, "I reckon. But one of y'all are gonna have to hike back here with me to get it."

Clarence walked back toward them.

Trainwreck wrapped the .45 in the plastic grocery bag he'd packed it in. He tied the mouth of the bag tightly closed and walked over to a large hickory tree six feet off the trail. Davey had taught them all to identify a hickory by its ridged vertical bark pattern and the long, narrow leaflets that grew from each stalk. This particular hickory had two eye-like knots above a gaping cavity in its trunk, which Joey imagined was the open mouth of an ancient wise-man sharing secrets with the brave souls who would journey many long, hard miles to seek his counsel. Inside that hole, Trainwreck placed the bag and covered it with leaves and twigs.

"There," he said to Clarence, clapping the dirt off his hands and wiping them on his jeans. From his pack, he pulled out the survival knife, sheathed in black, and strapped it to his thigh. "We come back for the gun next weekend. But you better hope we don't end up needing it on this trip or you're gonna look like a giant jackass."

The Bobcats continued their hike.

Chapter 10 – Meet the Goldsteins

The Goldstein family never expected the Cleaver to be coming.

While standing over a hot stove with one-year-old Georgie in her arms, Brenda Goldstein stared at the skillet and grumbled, "Damn it."

The TV commercial had lied. She'd purchased the new copper skillet based on the video demonstrating its marvelous non-stick surface, on which you could fry eggs that would slide freely around the pan like large lumps of mercury. It looked perfect for her foray into gourmet cooking. This revolutionary copper pan, claimed the television ad, could sauté vegetables, griddle pancakes, blacken fish, all with no pesky adhesion or related mess. You'd never even need to oil the pan with its dazzling new no-stick technology. When it came time to do the dishes—cleanup would be practically *effortless*!

Well, those claims held true for about two weeks, and then food started sticking to the thing like any other crummy old frying pan. Some *wonder* product. What's worse, the pan seemed to have warped from the heat, with the bottom bowed outward from the mid-point. Now it wouldn't cook evenly, which was critical for making the "perfect omelet" she'd promised Roland, due home any minute from work. The pan pooled the oil and turned what should have been a lovely dish into a scrambled mess, and scrambled eggs weren't on the menu. Brenda stood firm on this point.

Making things more difficult was the challenge of cooking dinner one-handed while carrying a baby. The nanny had the night off.

"Honey, I'm going to have to put you down for a sec."

Despite her blue-eyed boy's grunts and grapples, Brenda bent down and placed Georgie on the floor, then pivoted to a kitchen cabinet to dig out a different pan. As soon as she did this, Georgie let out a high-pitched squeal and launched into a crying fit. Right on cue.

As she hauled out an old skillet—a flat one, at least—the front door opened, and Roland stepped into the foyer of their open-floor lower level.

"Hi, hon," she said with a raised voice to carry through Georgie's screaming.

"Hey, babe," he answered. Then, in a sing-song fashion, he added, "Hey, Geoooooorgie!"

His son ignored him and continued to scream.

Roland placed his laptop bag beside the door and walked into the kitchen while loosening his tie. He approached Brenda from behind and kissed her cheek as she poured oil from one pan into the other.

"Let me change clothes real quick," he said in her ear. "I'll be right back."

To put a stop to all the hollering, Brenda scooped up Georgie and returned to the counter to crack eggs, one-handed.

#

Along the southern horizon, dark clouds gathered and thundered.

Wonderful, thought C.D. as he fumbled for another cigarette. *Things are going to get messy.*

The Cleaver had remained an implacable slab of granite throughout the entire drive to Hillbrook Heights, where every house was enormous in scale, modern in design, and immaculately maintained. Each yard consisted of a flawless green lawn highlighted by lush, symmetrical topiary…and C.D. hated every bit of it. He punched a code into the keypad at a security gate, which slid apart robotically, granting him access to bourgeois hell—enemy territory—the turf of wealthy snobs, crooked lawyers, and greedy politicians. When it came to these high-dollar homes, if he couldn't have one, it would suit him just fine to see them all burn to the ground.

"Fancy digs, huh?" he said mostly to himself.

He didn't bother to look at the Cleaver for a response and instead peered down at the papers Heidecker had given him, which had all the pertinent information for the job. They were searching for street number 1726. The mailbox that passed on the driver's side read 1722.

The Ford's dashboard clock read 6:32 p.m. As they approached the next house, he saw a Mercedes pull into the driveway as a garage door rolled open. The rush hour was fading, and people were arriving home from work, donning their slippers and preparing for dinner. Windows glowed in every house, and decorative wrought-iron streetlights bathed every block in a warm, burglar-discouraging radiance that one could only find in the ritziest areas of town.

The numbers 1726 reflected in the headlights from the brick mailbox of the next lot. C.D. slowed the SUV to a crawl and scoped the place through the tinted windows—a grand Federal Colonial sided with the same matching beige brick as the mailbox.

A slim brunette stepped out the front door. Goldstein's wife or daughter? She carried a baby in one arm and a skillet in the other. She stomped down the brick steps and followed a walkway around the side of the house. Approaching a waste bin tucked against the wall, she flipped open the lid with the frying pan and slam-dunked the skillet down inside the bin. After closing the lid, she marched back up the steps.

"She must have burnt the beans," C.D. said.

Before she entered the house, she turned toward the Expedition, which C.D. had brought to a near standstill without realizing it. He hit the accelerator to nudge the Ford past her house.

He turned to the Cleaver, obscured in his seat by all the hair and shadow, and asked, "What now?"

The Cleaver looked out the passenger window and stared down an adjacent street. C.D. kept the Ford at idle speed, but a pair of headlights approached from the rear, and he'd soon be forced to make a decision. Finally, the Cleaver pointed a finger at the roof of the car and moved it in a circling motion. C.D.

interpreted that as the universal sign for "go somewhere else," so he steered the SUV back toward the highway.

"Where to?" he asked.

The big, smelly bastard breathed deeply and grumbled a solitary word: "Motel."

About friggin' time, C.D thought. *So, the son of a bitch ain't mute after all.*

Chapter 11 – Get Ready

Trainwreck unzipped his fly.

"Hang on a minute. Don't pee there," Davey told him, tugging on the back of his friend's shirt. He pointed to the forest floor. "You know what that is?"

Trainwreck tucked himself back into his jeans and bent down to examine Davey's finding. "Yeah. It's called clover, genius. You see a four-leafer?"

Davey knelt next to him and plucked a pink flower along with some shamrock-shaped leaves from the bed of greenery. "It's not clover. You can tell because the flowers are trumpet-shaped. Clover flowers are round and sort of spiky."

The other boys gathered around to examine the specimen.

"So, what is it?" Trainwreck asked.

"It's oxalis." Davey shoved the palmful of weeds into his mouth and chewed them up. "The leaves and flowers are edible. You ever find yourself stranded in the middle of the woods, you can survive on wild plants, if you know what to look for."

Joey picked a leaf for closer inspection. "How do they taste?"

Davey's cheek swelled into a shifting lump as he rolled his tongue around his mouth. He grinned with green teeth. "Kind of bitter."

Davey selected a few more leaves and dug into his backpack. He pulled out a plastic sandwich baggie, placed the specimen inside, and Scotch-taped it into the binder containing the official Bobcat handbook.

"How's the book coming?" Paul asked him.

Trainwreck unzipped his fly once again. The others lined up along with him on the opposite side of the trail and unzipped too.

"Making progress," Davey answered. "Always working on it. Adding to it. Been trying to figure out a good Bobcat motto. Something simple that sums up what we stand for."

The Bobcats initiated their group peeing session, engaging in an unspoken contest of stream range. This round, Trainwreck came in first place for peeing the longest distance—a good eight feet—and Joey came in second. The winner of these games varied among the troops, but when it came to package size, Paul won every showing. They were all conscious of this, but no one ever spoke of it.

"What ideas you got for the motto?" Paul asked as they resumed their hike.

"Not much," Davey said. "I really like the Boy Scout motto, but that one's taken. Theirs is 'be prepared.' Short, sweet, and to the point."

"*Boy Scouts...*" Trainwreck said with a sneer. "Bunch of fashion victims."

Whereas the Boy Scouts required hideous green knee-socks and humiliating red neckerchiefs, the Bobcats were happy just to keep jelly off their shirt collars.

"Maybe we can just a re-word their motto," Paul said. "Make it our own."

"The easy way out," Joey said. "I like it. 'Be prepared'…We could just change that to 'Get Ready.'"

"Ready for what?" Trainwreck slapped a bug on his neck.

"Ready for anything," Joey said. "Ready for whatever the Boy Scouts are preparing for. Ready for whatever life throws at you. You got a math test coming up? *Get ready.* Playing a big basketball game this week? *Get ready.* Space aliens coming to invade the earth? *Get ready!*"

"Works for me," Clarence said.

"*Get ready,*" Davey said. "I don't hate it…"

The troop marched onward in a bout of silence until Trainwreck piped up with, "If space aliens were really about to invade, how would we get ready?"

The conversation that followed lasted more than an hour. As they hiked, they joked and they lied, and they spoke of their dreams of the years ahead. Davey the future veterinarian, Trainwreck the fireman, Clarence the scientist, and Paul the FBI investigator. Joey…well, Joey didn't know what he wanted to be. Maybe a writer.

Joey loved good books, video games, and pretty girls who turned his head, so those are things he brought to the conversation as the Bobcats scaled slippery rocks and hiked through thick underbrush.

Although he hated to admit it, he felt a different kind of freedom than he would have if his father had chaperoned the trip. As much as Joey admired the man, his dad had always maintained a serious demeanor. He was not a cold man—in fact, a truly generous sort—but he'd never been the life of the party, as though he always carried a mysterious burden.

Joey thought back to one Saturday when he'd taken their Cocker spaniel, Raleigh, out for a morning walk. He saw his dad digging holes across the street in Mrs. Butterman's yard on his day off. He'd lined a plot on her lawn with stakes and string, and the trailer hitched to his pickup was loaded with lumber. Joey didn't understand what he was doing, but since it looked like hard work, he slipped back inside the house to watch cartoons before being asked to help. Later in the day, he saw his dad nailing floorboards across a sloping frame of posts and joists in front of her house.

Joey walked over and asked, "What you doing, Dad?"

"Building a wheelchair ramp for Mrs. Butterman."

"Why?" Mrs. Butterman kept to herself, and aside from offering the obligatory roadside wave as she emptied her mailbox, Joey had had very little interaction with her. He didn't think his parents knew her well, either.

"Because she needs one."

That simple answer summed up his dad's outlook on life—one of voluntary responsibility. Joey later learned that Mrs. Butterman had fallen and injured her back. Although she'd never been particularly close with his parents, she was a neighbor, and that was close enough for his dad, who'd gotten word of the accident, saw a pressing need, and took action to answer it.

That was Joseph Kilgore in a nutshell: thoughtful, generous, admirable, and always willing to carry the burden for someone else. But Joey knew those burdens weighed on his dad and made him a serious sort.

So, being that his dad was never prone to silliness, Joey would have felt silly talking in front of him about things like his favorite mutant powers. He would have felt dumb seeing who could burp the loudest. Now, he and his friends could have important discussions about which girl in class had grown the biggest boobs.

Without his dad around, he was free of those second-guesses. Free to act young and unfettered.

His dad was not alone in his stoicism, of course. Heck, it seemed to Joey that all grown men were like that. When was the last time you saw a grown man skip down the sidewalk, roll down a grassy hill, or fall onto their back in an uncontrollable fit of the giggles? Joey figured somewhere along the way, that part of a man's life somehow faded away, or maybe those men all squeezed it out of their systems deliberately.

Why do that? To act like a kid was to spread wings of freedom, and to deny yourself that freedom was to die a little inside. Why would a man let something so beautiful die? Did youth die of old age, or did something eventually come along and killed it in the heart of every man?

Well, youth wasn't dead inside Joey. Not yet. He felt thankful for that as he grabbed a dangling vine and took a flying Tarzan-swing across a gully—complete with full-throated jungle wail. He threw the vine back to Davey, who caught it, grinned, and came soaring in Joey's direction with a brazen cry of complete abandon.

In the distance, thunder rumbled.

The weather system that had concerned his mother was building strength, licking its chops before it ate five young boys for dinner. The storm would be upon them soon, which meant they'd need to set up camp.

"I reckon it's gonna be a gully-washer," Trainwreck said loudly from the middle of the pack as they trudged up a hill. He bobbed his head to the music in his earbuds. "We better hunker down before she gets here."

At the head of the line, Joey encountered a waist-high mesh of tangled vines blocking the path. The overgrowth had been encroaching from either side of the trail.

"What's that smell?" Clarence said. The air held the rank odor of death.

Joey lifted a foot to kick through the bramble wall. The vines split with the force of his boot—and the brush exploded.

With a loud squawk, feathers and leaves clouded the air. Joey yelped and tumbled back into Paul who fell against Davey. They spilled to the ground, as three or four dark, flapping shapes ripped up from the forest floor and screeched into the air. Bursting through the branches above, the huge black birds disappeared deep into the reaches of the forest as debris showered the dogpile of seventh graders.

Stunned, Joey turned to Paul and Davey beneath him, both frozen with looks of surprise. As leaves drifted downward like confetti, Trainwreck let out a peal of laughter. Clarence joined him.

"Buzzards!" Trainwreck howled. "Holy crap, Kilgore, you look white as a sheet!"

Paul and Davey looked at Joey and broke out laughing. As Joey's heartbeat slowed its gallop, he rolled off his friends.

"Better check your undies, fellas." Trainwreck's trademark sprig of cowlicks wagged atop his head. "I know I'd better check mine."

Clarence wobbled on his backpack like an upturned turtle, clutching his ribs and chuckling.

Joey collected the spilled cooler, then stood and dusted himself off. The buzzards had been picking at the carcass of a small deer. The poor creature lay rotting with black, empty eyes, and Joey stared deep into those dark sockets and saw something stir.

"You okay, Joey?" Paul asked.

Joey tore his gaze away, but had a sudden uneasy feeling that the lifeless doe might be a bad omen.

The others waited for him to gather himself and retake his position at the head of their expedition. Which he did. He cleared his throat and spoke with his deepest voice and phoniest bravado, "Come on. Let's crest this hill and find a place to pitch camp."

He led them onward. The others followed, snickering.

Chapter 12 – Dusk

C.D. and the Cleaver each had a motel bed.

With his eyes on the television but his ears on the torture rack, C.D. tried to tune out the noise of the other man's whetstone as it scraped slowly down the blade, which stretched half the length of the mattress.

The Cleaver's bedspread lay cluttered with an array of custom-made weaponry. C.D. had initially marveled at the metal craftsmanship until the Cleaver had commenced his sharpening procedure, an endless nails-on-chalkboard kind of torment that would make any man's teeth clench. The blades were many and large—so damn large—some more than half the height of C.D., and the scraping was driving him mad.

#

Dinner for the Bobcats was a feast of Vienna sausages, cold-cut bologna, mixed nuts, dried bananas, and flour tortillas. The five of them ate and laughed around a campfire they'd surrounded with stones. Paul had brought a bag of marshmallows to roast skewered on sticks. The white treats glowed alight over dancing orange flames, then swelled, bubbled and blackened before the boys swallowed them down with delight.

Joey slapped a mosquito on his arm. It flattened into a bloody smudge. He leaned back against his bedroll with his legs outstretched. The others surrounded the fire likewise, patting their full bellies and heating their feet in a star-like pattern beneath the fading light while gazing up at the endless mystery of the heavens. Dusk brought the storm, bleeding a blacker darkness along the southern edge of the coming night. The weather would soon worsen.

Soon, but not yet.

Right now—these were the good times, and Joey didn't want to spend them lying down. Too restless to remain still, he stood from his spot and stretched his arms above his head. He turned to a large rock formation ten yards away, which overlooked a great hollow alongside the mountain—the view of which had helped to sell them on the campsite.

He climbed the rock face, and as he crested the top, the scenery took his breath. The world looked different. Now rested and fed, he gained a fresh perspective, and the mountaintop view left him awestruck. A part in the trees gave way to a beautiful spectacle of rolling hilltops and verdant treescapes stretched across the countryside with postcard perfection. The sunset had an otherworldly glow of tangerine ribbons that washed over the cloud-painted horizon with such a vastness that Joey felt microscopic beneath it. He couldn't understand how anyone could witness such natural beauty and deny the existence of God, or some sort of intelligent higher power. Because how could this all be an accident?

This is it, Joey thought, realizing the moment would never leave him. *This is living…making memories.*

Something clicked within his clockwork. Overcome with a deep feeling of acceptance, of rightness, he knew he belonged in that exact place at that very second with these close friends. And that piece of knowledge was a precious thing. This was what he'd journeyed here to find. It was what his dad had wanted him to learn from the trip—a final gift from father to son.

Joey didn't know much about anything, but he was learning. And, if he were pressed to share a single pearl of wisdom with anyone who might ask, it would be what he gathered here on the mountainside: to recognize that life is fast and fleeting, and the best of it boils down to a string of special moments shared with those few precious people with whom you form a lasting bond. He had to recognize those moments when they come, to drop everything, seize them, and drink them up for all their worth.

Joey planted his feet, took a deep breath of fresh Alabama air, and looked over the wondrous horizon. A drop of rain fell. Then a second drop hit his cheek. He tilted his face to the sky, opened his mouth, and did exactly as he would suggest. He drank up the moment. It tasted of honey and freedom.

The other Bobcats did the same. They lined up alongside Joey, facing the same pastoral beauty. They closed their eyes, tilted their heads, opened their mouths, and they drank.

#

Brenda Goldstein patted her face with a towel to blot away the excess moisturizer. When she dropped her hands, she saw Roland standing behind her in the bathroom mirror.

"Hey, Beautiful," he said with a wry smile. His favorite two words. It was his way of asking her to bed.

She liked the sound of those two words, as well as the implication, and returned the smile. "Hey, Handsome."

"I've got a surprise for you." He encircled her shoulders and lifted a necklace before her breast. The reflection of an ocean-blue pendant sparkled from a gold chain.

"My God, is that—?"

"Yep." He wrapped it around her neck. "Your birthstone."

"Sapphire? Oh my gosh!…" she said with a squeak of excitement, stroking the sizable gem with her finger and thumb. "It's so beautiful!"

"To match *you*, babe."

Brenda spun in his arms and hugged him. The shrimp and gouda omelet must have been a hit. She took his face in her hands and kissed him passionately, enjoying the touch of his warm skin, freshly smooth from a shave.

"I love it." She gazed into his eyes, hazel and sparkling with pride. "But I don't understand. You said…you know. Problems at work… We were going to have to cut back… How could you afford—"

"Shhhhh," he whispered and placed a finger to her lips. "Don't worry about it, babe. Things have turned around. I got a bonus."

"A bonus? You've never gotten a bonus. How did—"

"Shhhhh," he said again, then bent down and kissed her. "Just enjoy the moment."

For the time being, she decided to let it slide and do as he said. Tomorrow, she intended to find out how he came into money when he'd been so fretful about it the last two months, but that was tomorrow; this was tonight. So, when Roland flipped off the master-bath light and pulled her into the bedroom, she let out a giggle and surrendered to him completely.

#

The rain fell lightly at first, with the worst yet to come.

The boys climbed into the pup tents they'd arranged in a circle, lingering at the doors and watching the fire in the center hiss in the sprinkle. Joey saw Paul take out his photo of Candace and kiss it.

"You ever kiss her for real?" Trainwreck asked.

"You know he has," Davey said.

Paul only smiled.

"You ever done anything more than kiss her?" Trainwreck said with a gleam in his eye.

"That's none of your business," Paul said.

"Psssh. Figures."

"What figures?" Paul asked.

Trainwreck fluffed his pillow. "It figures that the only one of us with any girlie stories to tell would be Mr. Perfect. Mr. I-don't-kiss-and-tell."

Joey grinned. Trainwreck was right. If any of the other Bobcats had such a story to tell, they'd sky-write it, if that's what it took to make sure the other guys knew about it.

"Mr. Perfect?" Paul said. "What are you taking about?"

"Oh puh-*leeeaze*," Trainwreck said. "You got the movie star looks, the smokin' hot girlfriend, straight-A student, and you're the best hitter on the baseball team. It's disgusting."

Paul laughed. "We all got our different roles to play. I'm just the straight man. You're the loose cannon like Murdock on those old 'A-Team' reruns.."

Trainwreck grumbled to himself, "The loose cannon never gets the girl…"

The guys had a million questions for Paul about Candace Worton, and they pestered him relentlessly. Joey remembered the day she had sashayed into his and Paul's third-period science class. She had silky legs, golden skin, and eyes that could render a boy speechless. Most boys, but not Paul.

"How's it going?" Paul had whispered to the new girl after she was escorted by the teacher to the empty desk in front of him.

"Good, thanks," Candace had told him with an intoxicating smile, then turned in her seat to the head of the class.

Joey, who sat next to Paul, had gathered his courage and attempted the same, extending his hand. "I'm Joey Kilgore. Nice to meet you."

"Nice to meet you, Joey." She shook his hand, and he'd never felt skin so soft.

Not one to be outshined, Paul stuck his hand out too, and whispered, "I'm Bubba Drabowksi. Welcome to Trapper Valley."

Candace shook his hand and giggled. "I'm Candy. What kind of name is Bubba? Did your mom marry her brother?"

Joey stifled a laugh. This girl was a total firecracker.

"No," Paul said. "What kind of name is Candy? Do you dance naked around a pole?"

On hearing this, Joey nearly blew snot out of his nose, ducking down and muffling his laughter so Mrs. Wottle wouldn't notice. Boy, was Paul about to get an earful from the new girl.

Curling a lock of blonde hair around her finger, Candy had given a coy grin and said, "Maybe…"

Joey had almost died right then and there, right during Mrs. Wottle's lecture on photosynthesis. Paul's mouth fell open and his face flushed red. He cut his eyes at Joey, and both boys sank down into their seats with mile-wide smiles.

From that moment forward, a dreamy vision of Candy Worton dancing around a May pole fully nude and free would forever remain branded on Joey's imagination, and evidently on Paul's too. The couple hit it off. After a few meetups at the skating rink, Candy began going by Candace, and "Bubba" became Paul, the first and only Bobcat to have an honest-to-goodness *girlfriend*.

#

The Cleaver lay on his back in the motel room with a scarred forearm across his brow, concealing the eyes that could never be seen. The rise and fall of his chest gave the only indication he was still alive.

C.D. couldn't sleep. Hell, he couldn't even relax. To occupy his mind, he leaned against the headboard and watched animal documentaries on television.

He learned that female praying mantises often cannibalize their sex partners, sometimes beheading the poor chap before they've finished consummating the relationship. This reminded him of an old girlfriend.

He learned that vampire bats feed entirely on blood and that a hundred-bat colony will drink the blood of twenty-five cows every year. The bats reminded him of that bloodsucker Vinnie the Cat.

One show reported that bobcats are adept at bringing down animals that weigh several more times than they do, and are known to kill adult white-tail deer that weigh 250 pounds or more by jumping onto their back and biting through their throat.

With a bright flash, the TV switched to a laundry detergent commercial, but within that splash of light something odd caught C.D.'s eye. He squinted in the dark, then leaned over and twisted the switch on the bedside lamp. What he saw dropped his jaw.

He scrunched his brow in confusion, staring at the end of the Cleaver's bed, focusing on the man's hideous mammoth feet, hairy and calloused but with carefully painted pink toenails. Neon pink. The very last thing C.D. expected to see. He blinked his eyes to make sure it was no trick of the light.

"Can I ask you a question?" C.D. said to the Cleaver.

After a long stretch of silence, the Cleaver grumbled, "One." That single syllable seemed to echo deep within his chest.

One? thought C.D. with a shake of his head. *One question…Who the hell does this guy think he is?* C.D. easily had a dozen burning questions for the man. How'd you become a hitman? How'd you get hooked up with Heidecker? Why live in a shack in the woods? How many people have you killed?

"What's with the pink toenails?"

The Cleaver tilted his head beneath his beefy forearm and appeared to peer down the length of his body at his bare feet. He huffed air out through his nose, made a grumbling noise and smacked his teeth. With a low rattle in his voice as if he had a throatful of phlegm, he said, "Daughter painted them."

And with that response, C.D. suddenly had a hundred more questions, but he didn't ask them.

Chapter 13 – The Deep of Night

The hand on Joey's shoulder felt warm and recognizable. An old habit of his father's, that firm grip was a welcome ray of sunshine, a gesture of reassurance for Joey, who missed it dearly and would never forget the feeling. It meant he'd done a good job on reeling in that striped bass. It told him life would still go on after losing the spelling bee or missing a game-clenching bucket at the church-league basketball game. It meant everything would be okay.

"Enjoying yourself?" his father asked. He spoke in that low, husky voice with just a hint of Southern drawl which always comforted Joey and put him at ease.

"I love it here," Joey said.

They stood together side by side along the ledge atop the mountain ridge, marveling at the sprawling countryside which bristled with fantastical life. An army of butterflies—pink, orange, and yellow—fluttered in the thousands like confetti above the treetops. Great, majestic birds with silver feathers and twelve-foot wingspans soared in circles beneath golden clouds and distant stars that sparkled in the sunlight. A herd of white horses—could those be unicorns?—frolicked in the plains at the foot of the mountain. Those rolling plains had not been visible earlier in the evening.

"This is a special place, isn't it?" his dad asked.

Joey thought on this and decided that special failed to capture the awesome grandeur of this untamed world. "It's perfect."

"What have you learned while you've been out here?"

A white monkey with bright blue eyes swung onto the branch of a purple, smooth-barked tree with broad fan-like fronds. The monkey looked up the hill at them from below, gave an excited chitter, then leapt into a thicket, disappearing completely.

"I can think out here," Joey said. "I see things differently. I think I see what's important in life."

"You've gained a sense of clarity."

Joey rolled that word over, too. Clarity…as though everything was crystal-clear. But no, that didn't fit either. Nothing was clear. Life was only a little less foggy. Less cluttered. Out here in the wilderness, Joey found less distraction. He could focus on what mattered.

"I don't think I've gained clarity yet, but maybe I've found the path to get there. Maybe I'm pointed in the right direction."

His dad squeezed his shoulder, and Joey placed his hand over his father's.

"That's good," his dad said. "You have plenty of time to grow up and learn what works for you, but you're making progress, and that's what's important."

"Progress," Joey repeated to himself. It was a good word; fitting and hopeful. He remembered an old adage, one of his dad's favorites, that he now brushed off and gave back to him: "If you fall on your face, you're still moving forward."

"That's right. Just brush yourself off and keep on hiking. Progress…"

Thunder rumbled in the distance. The sky to the south darkened, and a shadow passed over the hillside. The clouds were golden no more, but gray, purple, and angry. A flash of light charged their edges with an electrical glow.

"Storm is coming," Joey said.

"Looks like it," his dad replied. "Things are turning dark." His father's voice seemed to echo when he said this.

"We'll be okay."

"Maybe," his father said, only the voice no longer sounded like Dad's. The word seemed to reverberate through the air, raspy, inhuman, and even reptilian.

Joey looked up at his father and shuddered. The man peered down at him with hollow, black eyes.

"Or maybe," said the thing who was not his father, "the path you're on will only grow darker."

Frozen at first by the sight of those missing eyes, Joey now stepped back. Something moved inside the dark corners of the lids and the edges of the mouth. Fine black hairs wriggled out of the sockets. Insect legs? No, these were strange, thin tendrils, inky and numerous.

"Maybe you're marching right into the gaping mouth of the beast," the distorted voice continued, growing agitated. "Maybe this journey leads to the end of the road. And maybe the darkness will spread like cancer, descend on you from above and devour you from below, worming its way inside your pores and saturating your soul, pumping it full of the stuff that runs through the Devil's veins."

Joey's breath caught in his chest, and he staggered backward.

"It eats you from the outside, and it eats you from within," the dad-thing continued in that ethereal voice, leaning into Joey with a crooked smile that leaked squirming, black appendages as something hideous struggled to free itself. "It will eat you alive just like it did me. Then pull you into a place so dark you'll long for the vibrance of the *grave. Your friends will all die too, but they won't die with you. All of them will die alone. Just like you. Alone, cold, stinking, and forgotten. In the black."*

"You're not my dad!"

"Oh, but I'm close enough," it grinned. "I am what your dad has become after death, little boy. Just a husk for things like me to play with."

Joey stumbled backward through the brambles, batting his hands to fend off the man with the living black syrup spilling from his eyes and lips—spilling cancer. At least, that was Joey's concept of the shit that killed his dad, an amorphous living venom that festered within someone like an alien parasite bent on consuming its host and everything around it.

Joey backed against a thicket of trees, the thick vines and briars blocking his escape. The dad-thing drew mere inches from his face.

"Now it's time," it said, "for me to play with your husk."

"Noooooo!" Joey screamed and bolted upright in his sleeping bag, shivering in a cold sweat. The night held him deep in its grip, and at first, he saw nothing.

"Dude, you okay!" Davey yelled from a neighboring tent.

"What's going on!" shouted Clarence, followed by the rustling of the Bobcats rousing from slumber and shoving out of their sleeping bags.

Joey's lungs had turned to ice. His fingers gripped the covers with such panicky strength that his knuckles hurt. The dad-thing was gone, but so was his dad—his *real* dad—gone forever, never to hug him or place that firm hand on his shoulder. Never again to reassure him, to guide him through muddy waters, never to offer the wisdom that Joey so desperately longed to hear from him. These were not new realizations, but suddenly all the darkness crashed over Joey with insufferable breadth and weight, suffocating him beneath a black dawn of loneliness, despair and an avalanche of regret—regret that he'd not said all the things he'd wanted to say to his father. Regret that he'd never heard all the things he'd wanted to hear from his old man. These thoughts tore a chasm through him, and he shrank there inside his tent and wept.

The tent flaps fluttered behind him, and a hand gripped his trembling shoulder. A thinner hand—Davey's.

"It's okay, bro," Davey said in a small voice. A kind voice, cautious but earnest.

"It's not okay," Joey blubbered through sobs. "It won't ever be okay! Nothing's ever gonna be okay again. Dad's gone. Gone forever! Why'd God have to do that to him? Why'd God have to take my dad? He was the best. My dad was the best, and what kind of God creates cancer? I mean, I've always believed in Him and in Jesus and love and the Bible and doing what's right. Dad taught me that! So why does this happen to him? 'Cause it ain't fair! It's not *fair*!"

"I know, man. It ain't fair. I mean, I don't know what to say, but I'm sorry." Davey's hand tightened on Joey to emphasize this.

Joey wiped his brow, catching his breath in the stuffiness of the tent's dew-laden air. The forest buzzed with legions of crickets.

A horrible dream, that's all it was, thought Joey. An ugly dream conjured by the ghosts he'd tamped down deep into the basement of his mind, hoping to keep them hidden and silent. But they'd broken free while he'd been asleep, screeching and howling and spreading the kind of pain that twists a soul like it's a dirty dishrag, wringing it dry of all hope and happiness, leaving it limp, withered, and ruined. That's how Joey felt right at the moment—gutted by his uncaring God and mocked by the ghosts of what would never be.

But it was just a dream, Joey reminded himself, reciting it in his mind like a magical chant that would ward away evil. *Just a dream.*

Despite God's refusal to protect his father, Joey knew the truth was that Dad walked with Jesus in Heaven. Joey had to believe it, that one day they'd join hands again in the afterlife. It was crucial to maintain faith, even though clinging to those ideas felt like gripping a burning rope as he dangled from a cliff. He would hold onto that belief no matter who told him otherwise or what ugly hand the world may deal him. Because, with that faith came hope, and without that hope the world beyond this one looked empty and bleak.

Nothing but a husk.

"Sorry," Joey, still in a daze, said to Davey. "I'm okay."

Davey relaxed his grip and patted Joey's back. "Holy cow,

man. I thought you were getting attacked."

Joey wiped away tears and looked at his friend, squinting at his red and blue Braves ball cap. "Do you sleep in that thing?"

"What's all the commotion?" Trainwreck muttered from somewhere outside.

Davey threw a glance over his shoulder. "I think Joey had a bad dream."

Davey was the newest of the crew, having moved to town only last summer. They'd met him as he held the front door open at school—for *everyone*. On his first day, this new kid in a Braves cap had opened the door for a teacher just as a train of young female students trailed her into the school, so he held it for them too. Then, more kids followed. He didn't want to be rude, so Davey ended up standing at door duty throughout the entire morning rush. The next day, he did the same (minus the hat, which he learned violated the dress code). Each morning he volunteered to be "that door-holding guy," having found an easy way to break the ice with the other kids.

Davey became a Bobcat the day the other four found him under siege on the playground at Black Creek Park. Scotty Heckler and three other locals had him cornered along a chain-link fence, calling him "Tonto" and throwing dirt clods at him. Joey, Trainwreck, Paul and Clarence recognized "the door-holding guy"…and nobody likes a bully. Heckler and his idiot sidekicks soon hightailed it out of there, fleeing an onslaught of earthen missiles and mortars, courtesy of the Bobcats. Davey and the gang became fast friends, and Joey had learned that— newest or not—when times were tough, Davey would be the first guy in your corner with a shoulder to lean on and an ear to listen.

"Bad dream?" Trainwreck said. "Y'all disturbed my beauty sleep over a cotton-pickin' nightmare?"

"Don't say 'cotton-picking,'" Clarence chimed in. "It's racist."

"Give me a break…" Trainwreck said with an air of dismissal.

Davey stuck his head outside and whispered to the others, "I think it was about Mr. K."

For a long moment, they all remained silent.

Finally, Trainwreck said, "What time is it?"

Clarence checked his phone and said, "It's 11:11… Fart in your hand and make a wish!"

Trainwreck groaned. "I wish I were back asleep." After a moment he said, "That's rotten what happened to your dad, Joey. We all loved him."

Joey sniffled and crawled out of his tent for some fresh air. The others were huddled around the smoldering campfire. The ground was soaked but the rain had ceased for the moment.

"He's right, you know," Paul added, scratching his ear. "All of us thought the world of Mr. K."

Joey nodded. "Thanks for saying that."

"Fuck cancer," Trainwreck said.

The others all looked at him.

Swearing was not uncommon, but the F-word was the big

gun, and the Bobcats almost never used it. Joey figured if anything ever deserved that venom, it was cancer. A fury stirred inside of him.

"Yeah," Joey said. "Fuck cancer."

"Fuck cancer!" Davey shouted.

The trees above them rustled with wildlife.

"Fuck cancer." Paul growled it with gravel in his voice, the way Joey had seen cowboys sneer their lines in old western movies.

Clarence stood up from his seat on a log, put his hands to his mouth like a bullhorn, and screamed at the sky: "Fuck fucking *cancer!*"

Joey, rising to his feet, demanded the same of the heavens above: "Fuck you, cancer! Fucking *die!*"

Each of the Bobcats stood and shouted the battle cry, screaming, cursing, releasing the pent-up anger the disease so rightly deserved. They blasted their hearts free of the pressure that had been building inside from the painful memory of what happened to Mr. K., spewing out the adolescent rage that fuels and plagues the years of youth and feeling much cleaner from the catharsis.

After the barrage of profanity diminished, the five boys laughed at each other and climbed back inside their tents, with Davey and Clarence sharing one together. They curled up in their sleeping bags but kept their heads at the tent flaps to keep up the camaraderie, now that they'd been sufficiently disturbed from sleep.

"Dang, Joey," said Trainwreck, as he tore the plastic off a

strip of beef jerky. "The way you cried out, I thought Jason Voorhees done got ahold of you."

"Or Michael Myers," Paul added.

"Or Freddy Krueger," said Davey, "or Victor Crowley!"

"Or the Leprechaun," Clarence added, only for Trainwreck to belt out a laugh at his suggestion.

"The Leprechaun…" Trainwreck said in a muse. He rolled onto his back and gazed up at the sky muted matte black by unseen clouds. "What would you guys do if one of those suckers was after you?"

"Who, the Leprechaun?" Clarence asked.

"Any of 'em," Trainwreck said. "If there was a maniac hunting us out here in the woods, what would you do? Run? Fight?"

"Call a forest ranger," Clarence said. He held up his phone.

"You still getting reception out here?" Paul asked him.

Clarence looked at his phone and scrunched up his brow. "Oh. No. Crap."

"That was a dumb answer, anyway," Trainwreck said. "You know the phone number of the closest forest ranger? No. Besides, you wouldn't have time for anybody to rescue you before you got chopped into dog food."

"Fine, genius," Clarence said. "What would *you* do?"

"Shoot him."

Clarence didn't reply to that.

"Then burn him," Davey said.

The others laughed.

"Wow," Paul said. "Bobcats are brutal."

"No, Davey's right," Trainwreck said. "You can't take any chances in a situation like that. You got to make sure it's final. I mean, the killer *always* comes back. You got to make sure they can't come back for the sequel. I'd cut him up into little pieces. At least cut off their head."

"That ought to do it," Joey said. "When chased by a crazed killer, first shoot 'em. Then cut off their head. Then set them on fire."

"Sounds like a plan." Trainwreck craned his head to look at the others. "Davey, make sure to write that down in the Bobcat handbook."

Davey did exactly that.

Chapter 14 – The Job

With a sharp bang, the mattress jolted beneath C.D. and startled him awake. He'd drifted off watching television, and now the Cleaver loomed at the foot of his bed, having kicked the frame with a big, booted foot.

"Let's go," he commanded.

The keys to the Expedition landed on C.D.'s chest with a thump and slid into his armpit.

Trying to adjust his eyes to the dark room with a flashing television, C.D. squinted at the bedside clock radio. It read 2:12 a.m. The Cleaver, boots on and laced, opened the motel door and bent down to walk through it, into the night.

"Damn it," C.D. muttered.

The fog of sleep always took him a few minutes to shake away. He leaned over, dropped his feet to the floor, and sat on the edge of the mattress with his forehead cradled in his hands. Where were they, again? Oh yeah, a cheap motel up the highway from the Hillbrook Heights exit. He was here to do a job, like it or not.

C.D. pulled on his leather chukka boots and doubled the knots. He yawned, stretched, and stood up. By the time he'd shoved his wallet and car keys into his pockets and grabbed his coat, the Cleaver was back at the door, filling it with his monstrous frame.

"*Now*," the man grumbled, then left again.

C.D. hated the impatient son of a bitch and would be counting the hours until he could ditch him back in the forest and never see this asshole again.

#

Brenda Goldstein awoke in the dead of night, unsure of what had disturbed her. Had it been a noise? A car door? Some unfamiliar clank of metal? She didn't know but didn't think it mattered. That was one of the wonderful things about Roland — he was an ample provider. He'd bought them a house in Hillbrook Heights, gated and secured in a posh community far too exclusive for the residents to worry about common street crime, burglaries, and the like. The only bad element she had to fear were the local teens drinking too much and driving too fast in their sports cars. But still…something felt slightly *off* tonight. Brenda knew she'd never get back to sleep without checking on Georgie.

Roland was snoring beside her. No need to wake him. She could take care of this herself, maybe get a glass of water while she was up. Maybe even sneak a cookie.

She looked for the clock-radio on the nightstand, but the glowing digits were nowhere to be seen. Had Roland moved the clock? She grabbed her phone from the tabletop. It read 2:55. Five minutes until the "devil's hour," she recalled hearing from some obscure snippet of horror movie dialogue.

Stepping into the hallway and feeling a chill, she rubbed her shoulders. Roland must have turned down the thermostat before bed. Gooseflesh rose on her arms. The house felt drafty, and she tried to remember if she'd opened a window earlier in the day and perhaps had forgotten to close it.

The hallway was exceptionally dark. It took a moment to register that the staircase was missing the muted brilliance from the kitchen light on the lower level, which they left on for late-night excursions, exactly like this one—a common occurrence when you had a temperamental baby. They'd probably turned off the light by mistake. The windows glowed orange from the streetlamps, suggesting there hadn't been a neighborhood power outage, so maybe she and Roland had simply been forgetful.

If ever there was a good excuse to be forgetful, they'd had a great one, she thought with a smile.

She passed the staircase and slipped into Georgie's room, tapping the phone so the screen brightened to guide her toward the wooden crib. Georgie sat waiting upright and fully awake. Something had disturbed him too. As Brenda approached, his eyes lit up, and he reached for her and cooed. She lifted him, kissed him, and carried him to get a bottle of milk, thankful her breastfeeding days were over.

Using the dim light of her phone, she swept down the steps and whisked into the kitchen, pulling open the refrigerator door to a black interior. The fridge's light didn't come on. She couldn't hear its characteristic hum. The power to the house must be off. She pulled out the milk and set the jug on the counter.

A cool breeze tickled her skin and brought with it a rank, feral odor. She looked past the kitchen at the front door, which stood ajar. That breeze. The odor. Someone, or something, had entered the house. She tightened her hug around Georgie.

"Honey?" Roland said from the top of the staircase.

With a series of arhythmical thumps, he padded down the stairs as Brenda sensed unseen movement somewhere nearby, somewhere deep within the shadows of their house. Brenda scoured the dark corners and spans of wall between the front windows, searching for any sign of an intruder. The open-floor bottom level provided many places to hide between the shafts of tawny light streaming from outside.

"Why are the lights off?" Roland asked. "And what's that smell?"

"I don't know," she whispered, but didn't know why. "I think someone's in the house."

Roland crept over to the door and examined the jamb. The casing was broken. "Someone kicked it in."

That must have been the noise that woke her. "Shouldn't the alarm have sounded?"

"Maybe not if the power's been cut," he said. "But we've got a backup battery. Should be alerting the police right now."

From a dark corner to the left of Roland, a shadow emerged and towered over him. Roland spun with a gasp and staggered back into the foyer. Silhouetted against the window like a living, breathing nightmare, something humanoid, but larger and beastly, lifted a huge band of metal above him. Light glinted off the thick, sharpened steel.

Brenda's breath caught in her throat. Roland twisted back in her direction, and she'd never seen his eyes so wide, his expression so panicked. She screamed his name.

Georgie screeched.

So fast, the blade fell. Roland's head cocked back, and his lips parted. A great metal edge hacked deep through his shoulder, down through his chest, and nearly to his navel, seizing him in mid-stride.

Brenda's stomach rolled as blood splashed to the floor.

Roland's shoulder gaped open from his torso like a lightning-stricken tree trunk splitting along the grain.

The man-beast ripped the blade out of her husband's back. Roland spilled forward and sprawled facedown with a weak, heaving noise. The caveman wielded a monstrous axe-handled cleaving blade, at least three feet long and a good eight inches wide. It dripped with blood.

Georgie's squall pierced her ear. Brenda's head quaked. Which way to run? The kitchen island stood between herself and the killer, who now stalked toward her, cast in the pale glow of her phone. She backed up against the stovetop.

He approached the island barstools, kicked them aside, then swiped the blade in a vicious arc across the tabletop. Brenda drew back and felt the air wisp from the slice. Instinctively, she lunged in the opposite direction from which he swung. If she could make it past him and sprint to the door, she could dash outside and scream for help.

With Georgie bunched beneath her arm like a football, she took off around the corner. Mere inches to spare, she escaped the man's clutching hand, stumbling from the kitchen to the foyer.

Only fifteen feet to the door.

Then, her foot slipped. Her leg gave way. She lost traction, slamming onto her side into a hot pool of Roland's spreading blood. Pain wracked her elbow. With Georgie squawking beneath her, Brenda scrambled to her hands and knees, slipping and sliding. As she shoved upward, something struck her neck.

Her vision spiraled. The world reeled like the film of an old movie projector. The windows flashed, and shapes blurred. Her head smacked onto the floor and rolled to see the stump of her neck pump blood in a slowing beat.

Georgie squirmed on the floor in the glow of her phone, as the killer raised a heavy boot above her precious young son.

All went black.

Brenda never heard the crunch.

#

As he sat curbside in the Expedition waiting on his partner to complete the grisly assignment, C.D. felt like his entire nervous system was a network of steel wire being cinched tighter by the minute. On the way to the mark, the Cleaver hadn't spoken a word of his plan or his method. He'd gotten out of the vehicle, opened the hatch, hauled out his duffel, and disappeared in the direction of the Goldstein house.

So, C.D. had waited until he'd heard a sharp *CRACK!* He

glanced over to see that Mr. Personality had kicked the house's front door open like the most brainless amateur C.D. had ever seen. Any fool could tell you that a place so upscale had a security system, the kind with redundancies that alert the cops even if—and especially when—the circuit is disconnected. Although C.D. couldn't readily hear the shriek of an alarm, he knew the sirens would soon be screaming toward them.

There he sat like a hapless fool, knowing he'd be dead if he were to split before they'd completed the assignment. Yet with each ticking second, he felt more destined for the slammer.

As C.D.'s gaze ping-ponged back and forth from the Goldstein's front door to the dashboard clock—3:10…3:11…3:12. The Cleaver finally emerged from the darkness with the duffel on one shoulder and a bulging plastic bundle beneath the other. He shoved both items into the back of the Expedition, then returned to the house.

That's when C.D. heard the dreaded high song of a police siren from somewhere up the highway. He gripped the steering wheel and swore another silent oath of vengeance against Vinnie the Cat. The Cleaver's shadow appeared again with two larger objects hoisted onto each shoulder. As he passed the window, C.D. saw they were wrapped in black plastic sheeting. The Cleaver shoved them lengthwise through the back hatch, slammed it, then came around and climbed into the Ford.

C.D. tried to act calm as he shifted into gear, but as soon as the Cleaver shut his door, he pegged the gas, chirped the tires, and shot out of the neighborhood, nearing something like warp speed. Out on the main road, the local pigs were racing in their direction—three cruisers bumper to bumper with cherries blazing. C.D. slowed and passed them casually in the opposite direction without incident.

Holy shit, I'm gonna die of a heart attack, is what he thought.

Soon, he was heading back toward the mountain forest to some remote location where the Cleaver insisted on dumping the bodies. C.D. felt calmer and more confident about the situation. Maybe, just maybe, he'd get out of this pickle a free man…and with his skin intact.

Chapter 15 – Saturday Morning

The birds greeted the dawn with a cheerful song of musical peeps and merry chirps. The rain had drizzled but yet to downpour, and Joey could tell from the glow of his tent canvas the sun was peeking through the clouds. He yawned and stretched and crawled outside to the smoldering ash pile in the center of their circle.

Clarence was awake and sitting fireside, munching on crumbled Pop Tarts from a Ziploc freezer bag. "Pah Tah?" he offered with his mouth full of crumbs.

"No thanks," Joey said.

Trainwreck crawled out of his tent and stumbled over a log. He sneezed, spat in the grass, and rubbed his eyes with balled fists. His two cowlicks twitched in the wind as if searching for radio reception.

Paul emerged from his tent and yawned like a bear. He made an athletic display of stretching his arms and thighs.

Davey was the last to join them, already dressed in his hat, boots, and a rain slicker. He was brighter-eyed than the others. "What's up, ladies?"

"Got a bag full of Pop Tarts if anybody wants some," Clarence offered, smacking his lips.

Trainwreck farted in reply then turned to a tree and took a leak.

Joey looked up through the leaves. A ray of sun peeked

through a slice in the clouds, but the surrounding clouds were closing it off like a wound healing in dead skin. Once the bottom fell out of those clouds, they'd not only have to contend with the water overhead but more slop underfoot. The path would become ever more treacherous, and mudslides would pose a serious hazard.

"Maybe we ought to eat breakfast while we walk," Joey said. "Better make some headway before more rain hits. When it does, it's really gonna slow our progress."

Clarence popped a palmful of frosted tart into his mouth and shrugged. "Suits me. You're the boss."

This struck Joey as odd. Maybe Clarence intended it as a figure of speech, but Joey had never considered himself to be the boss of anything.

The Bobcats broke down their tents, squeezed the air from their canvases, wrestled them into tight rolls, and commenced to cramming them back into their respective travel tubes. Only Davey managed this task successfully, while the others settled with leaving the loose ends of their unstuffed tent-rolls bulging from their backpacks like hernias.

Joey pulled the map from his pack, and they all reviewed it in a huddle. As long as they stuck to the schedule, they should make it to Lonesome Bridge—the halfway point of their trip— shortly after noon.

Onward they hiked, refreshed, happy, and enthusiastic.

#

Why take the stiffs back to the mountain?

C.D. shifted the Expedition into four-wheel drive to negotiate a washed-out, rock-laden path up Black Oak Mountain. They were back in Cleaver country, and it didn't make a lick of sense to C.D. why the man would want to stash the bodies anywhere close to his home, but he assumed Mr. Pink Toes was insane, so he didn't bother him with any questions. As instructed, C.D. followed this road to nowhere, which further delayed completion of their mission.

Don't that just figure, he thought.

As soon as this job ended, he planned to treat himself with a trip to see Cindy. *Sin-dee,* as he thought of her, was a working girl in Birmingham, a real sweet one with a full chest, pouty lips, and a warm bed whenever he needed to unwind. And C.D. desperately needed to unwind.

He lit another cigarette.

#

The terrible thing the Bobcats saw at the bottom of the cliff was enough to throw cold water onto those red-hot coals of youth.

They were winding along a western ledge, which dipped to a lower elevation above a sheer cliff face where weeds and saplings grew, thinning the tree cover and granting a partial view of the sprawl down the mountainside. As they approached the clearing, Joey heard a car door close. Assuming they were miles from a proper roadway, this had sparked his interest, and the others followed him to the precipice where he saw movement down below.

Someone maybe a hundred feet down the mountain, partly obscured by branches and leaves, reached two muscular arms into the hatchback of a black SUV. He dragged out an oblong shape wrapped in black plastic, and a thin, lifeless arm spilled out of it.

Clarence gasped.

The plastic bundle slapped to the ground beneath the layered branches of the encroaching trees. The mysterious figure, all hair and muscle like a genuine bigfoot, lifted the bundle and appeared to heave it into the side of the mountain. He returned to the vehicle from beneath the mesh of leaves and hauled out another black-wrapped shape. Joey's throat went dry.

On the third trip to the truck, the figure dragged out a much smaller plastic-wrapped package, this one dwarfed by those massive forearms.

Any lingering spark inside Joey went cold at that very moment. He knew at that instant his childhood had been snuffed out just like the baby in the bag. For no flame could flicker beneath the growing sense of suffocation that now seemed to press on him from above, from below, and from every surrounding direction.

"Oh my god," Clarence whispered.

The others remained silent.

Down below, the small package and the big figure vanished from sight.

For a long moment, the world was quiet. Even the dripping rain seemed to hush. Nothing but the driving beat of Joey's heart pounding in his ears.

With both hands, Clarence lifted his phone before him to focus its camera. "We need evidence." But when he stepped forward for a better view, the ground gave way. "Shit!" he said, losing his footing and sliding toward the cliff's edge.

Joey snatched Clarence's shirt sleeve, as Paul hooked an arm around him, scooping him backward and onto solid soil. Clarence pounded down in a sitting position, phone still in his fingertips. A cascade of mud and rock slid loose and tumbled off the ledge, bouncing down the sheer hillside.

Joey held his breath and prayed the patter of falling rain had covered the noise. He peered back over the ledge and found the stranger staring up and pointing them out for someone else—someone who now stood next to the driver's door with a pistol in hand.

"They notice us?" Clarence asked.

Davey and Trainwreck each had a handful of tree branch to secure themselves as they craned their necks to see below.

The men at the bottom exchanged angry shouts, then shots rang out.

Davey and Trainwreck flew backward with a cry. In a flash, Joey grabbed Clarence and, with Paul's help, heaved him off the ground. They stumbled through weeds and broke into a mad sprint up the trail. Two more gunshots cracked through the forest behind them.

"They're really shooting!" Trainwreck yelled. "Holy crap!"

"Just run!" Joey shouted. "Run!"

The Bobcats blazed a trail at record speed, ripping knees through thistle and hedge like plow blades, fueled by fear and the pure instinct of self-preservation.

"How many did you see?" Paul asked. "How many people?"

"Only saw two," Trainwreck said.

Clarence, already panting and favoring a limp, slowed his pace. "Guys, hold up a minute!"

Trainwreck shot a glance behind him and growled, "No time! Run!"

"Guys—where's Davey?" Clarence asked.

Everyone hitched their stride and stared at Clarence, who slowly turned to look back down the path.

"Oh no," he said.

Joey's heart sank.

Clarence planted his feet, took a deep breath, then charged back down the trail in the direction they had come.

The other Bobcats looked at one another. Nothing needed to be said. They all dashed after Clarence.

#

"Shoot them."

The Cleaver's command had been simple enough to understand, but it fell beyond the job description of a guy like C.D., who was always eager to scam an easy dollar but didn't like to play rough unless absolutely necessary. And when it came to killing kids, C.D. didn't think he could ever deem that necessary. Hell, he'd never shot anyone, and he wasn't going to start with children.

Those were kids who'd spotted them at the top of the cliff — he could see that plain as day. Yeah, it was bad news they'd been seen hiding the bodies, but this problem could be fixed without more bloodshed. Why was this asshole so fixated on hiding the corpses in a cave? They could find a new dump location and be halfway across the state before the kids ever squealed to the cops.

Besides, C.D. had been hired as a driver, not an assassin, and not as a little bitch errand-boy like this Cleaver bastard seemed to think.

"I don't shoot kids," C.D. told him.

From the mouth of the cave, the Cleaver advanced on C.D. with murder in his face. He rounded the Expedition with those monstrous hands outstretched and fingers hooked like talons.

"Okay—*shit!*" Rather than die, C.D. obeyed orders. He thrust his nine-millimeter into the air and fired several rounds uphill in the general direction of the kids.

The Cleaver stopped advancing. "Kill them all."

Fuming, C.D. stretched out his arm again and fired twice

more. He didn't exactly aim and secretly hoped the kids had scrammed, that he'd missed them, but he needed to keep this murdering son of a bitch off his back for just a little while longer.

"Chase them down," the Cleaver said.

"What?" C.D. said. "Are you friggin' kidding me?"

"*Now.*"

Hot air streamed from C.D.'s nostrils. He stamped his foot and paced in a circle. He checked his magazine then slammed it back into the grip. "*Fuck!*" he said, making his way toward the bottom of the incline and wondering just how in hell he was supposed to climb to the top of the ledge.

#

By the time the other Bobcats caught up with him, Clarence was kneeling over Davey with two fingers on his neck. Davey lay on his back where he'd fallen in the mud. His Braves hat lay beside him. Blood stained the left side of his forehead and a spot on his chest. The Bobcats watched Clarence, awaiting the news.

After a moment, Clarence's head dropped. His shoulders shuddered, and he leaned onto Davey's chest and covered his face with folded arms.

Then, Davey coughed.

Clarence bolted upright. "Oh, thank God!"

"He's gonna be okay, ain't he?" Trainwreck asked with a waver in his voice from over Clarence's shoulder. "Davey, buddy, you okay?"

"Has he really been shot?" Paul asked.

Joey's hand went to Trainwreck's shoulder. Paul took a knee next to Clarence. They all hovered around Davey, whose body trembled, lips moving with effort.

"Take it easy, man," Clarence told him. "Don't try to talk. Somebody get him some water. Davey, just relax. Paul, get me a rag or something to apply pressure to the wound."

"Pressure to the wound." The phrase snapped Joey from a daze.

They'd all studied first aid as Bobcats. His Dad had shown the pack some basics, but it was Davey who'd set up some actual triage drills so they could practice their skills. They'd made fake blood from Karo syrup and used sausage links as exposed intestines. This time, Davey's blood was real.

"Take the buh…," Davey strained to say with his eyes half closed, tapping at the strap of his backpack. "Take the buh…"

"What is it, buddy?" Clarence said. "What do you want?"

"Take the buh…" Davey said weakly.

"The backpack?" Paul said. "Take your backpack? We'll take care of it, don't worry."

"The buh…"

"The book?" Joey said. He took Davey's hand and squeezed it. "The Bobcat book you've been working on? That what you mean?"

"The buhhhhh…."

This time, the breath that left Davey's lips did not return again. His grip went limp in Joey's hand.

Joey swallowed hard and backed up against a tree.

"Oh no," Clarence gasped.

"He can't be…" Trainwreck began, voice cracking. "I mean, he ain't really?…" He staggered a few feet, grabbed his knees and gave a dry heave.

Everyone knew the truth, but nobody had an answer for Trainwreck. Joey felt numb, small and lost in a dizzying world that seemed to have spun right out of orbit within such a small slash of time.

Thunder crashed and wind roared. The trees around them bent with whipping branches. Joey gazed up at the angry sky rolling in, as though all of creation had been tilted, and the clouds were sliding downhill.

"I can't believe this," Paul said in whisper.

"We…" Clarence began with a whimper. Tears streamed down his face. "We can't just leave him here."

"Of course not," Joey heard himself say. "Bobcats are loyal."

"Take off his pack," Paul said. "I'll carry it."

Trainwreck had walked back to the ledge. "Fellas," he said, peering downhill and to his left. "They're climbing up the mountain after us."

A shiver coursed through Joey.

"Oh crap." Clarence rose to his feet. "What do we do?"

"The bridge can't be far," Paul said. "Right, Joey?"

"Shouldn't be too far…" Joey said with a million thoughts and fears racing through his head. Joey had only seen Lonesome Bridge in his dad's old photos and in his many dreams since. A suspended steel-rope and plank structure that crossed a great ravine, it represented more than the last leg of their journey. The trail on the other side was said to scale downhill, which would hasten their escape.

"We got a good head start, but we better run like hell," Trainwreck said.

"What about Davey?" Paul asked.

Trainwreck wiped his eyes then dropped his pack. He tore into the pouch and fished out a rope. He ran over to Davey, pushed the backpack aside, and began working the rope beneath his back to form a loop.

"What are you doing?" Clarence said.

"We can't carry Davey if we're being chased," Trainwreck said. "We gotta leave him here and come back later. This will keep the animals off him. Help me, please!"

Trainwreck acted fast, and what he said cut through a dense fog and made sense to Joey, who needed specific directions on what to do with his hands and body. In no time, they had the other end of the rope draping a thick tree branch, onto which they hoisted up their dead friend. His soaking clothes made him heavy, and it took four Bobcats to hang him high.

"We better go," Paul said, strapping Davey's backpack over his shoulder and on top of his own.

Back at the ledge to check their pursuers' progress up the incline, Trainwreck yelled to the others over the hiss of rain, "I don't see anyone!"

Clarence turned to Joey, as if for instructions. "That's bad."

Joey looked at Davey up in the tree, the bill of his baseball hat pulled down to cover his face. Nothing but a husk. It felt so disrespectful. But Trainwreck had been right. They would have to come back.

"Let's go," Joey said.

The four remaining Bobcats followed Joey, battling their way up the trail through brushwood, vine, and vicious wind and rain.

Chapter 16 – The Slog

"That bastard piece of shit!" C.D. seethed.

He tried to wedge one of his 300-dollar leather chukkas against a protruding root, while pulling himself up a steep rut by gripping a sapling. That craggy crevice was the only place uncovered by foliage where he could get a decent foothold, but there was no place to secure a handhold. As he labored, he cursed the Cleaver, and Heidecker, and Vinnie the Cat, and those three fuckers who'd robbed him, along with any of their no-good friends and relatives—*Let 'em all get cancer!*

The branch in his fist tore out of the ground. He slipped into the rut and folded his ankle, then slid downhill.

"Oww, shit, dammit!"

At this point, he considered just saying *screw it*, climbing back down, starting the Ford, and leaving the big, hairy maniac alone in the woods. Let him track down those kids on his own. C.D. had only scaled maybe half the incline to reach the height where he'd seen the kids, and the effort had been sheer hell. Now his ankle was screaming, his clothes were soaked, and everything in his whole world caused him misery.

But what if the Cleaver was waiting down below? C.D. had seen the asshole head uphill in a parallel direction, carrying his sack of blades into the woods. What if he had turned back? What if the Cleaver was now waiting casually back at the Expedition, clipping his pink toenails while C.D. played the patsy, hunting down children through the Alabama backwoods?

If C.D. encountered him back at the car, there would be a confrontation. C.D. would have to shoot him or face the wrath of those huge, homemade blades. Hell, maybe the Cleaver even had a gun of his own stashed in that duffel bag. A gunfight with a seasoned killer appealed even less to C.D. than climbing the muddy hill during a rainstorm. That's the scale he used to weigh his options, so he got back to climbing.

#

The Bobcats trudged as fast as they could through tangle and bush and sodden earth.

Trainwreck manned the end of the line, gritting his teeth as the magnitude of Davey's murder slowly burned into him like a coat of acid. Smiling Davey would never again hold the door open for him at school. He'd never again hold the door for anyone. The Injun with a Heart of Gold, as his Gramps might say—that was good ol' Davey, a Bobcat through and through. Davey would never conduct any more of their battlefield first-aid sessions. He'd never again teach the other guys which species of tree was which, or what animal left behind a funny-looking pile of turds. He'd never finish his ever-growing Bobcat handbook, which he held so dear to his heart. And all those accumulating *never agains* simmered inside Trainwreck with growing intensity.

Those piece-of-crap murderers had shot Davey right out of the blue, without a second of warning. It had been a total sucker punch—the ultimate act of cowardice. It only took a couple quick pulls of a trigger, and they'd stolen his youth, his dreams and his future, without so much as a thought. Killing Davey had been like swatting a fly to them. Now they were all just flies escaping the flyswatter.

Trainwreck's thoughts stoked the fire inside him, which replaced his sadness with a rising sense of indignation and fury. He held tight to that spark.

Because, for Trainwreck, sadness meant slowness. Pain could be paralyzing. This was no time to drag ass.

Here they were, four men running through the woods in full retreat from two others who'd just shot their friend, and if he and the other Bobcats didn't make it to safety, then they might just get shot too.

Yet, there was only so much solace to be sought with safety, and Trainwreck knew that simply running away would never be enough to stop what would haunt him in the years to come. What would haunt him would be *regret*—regret for not doing what he could have to even the score on Davey's behalf.

Trainwreck didn't much like running away. He didn't take well to getting pushed around. Nor did he like anybody messing with his friends. Especially the Bobcats.

Bobcats bite back.

These thoughts centered him and angered him. He clenched his fists to hold onto that anger, because anger could be empowering.

Trainwreck lifted his gaze from the ground he'd been staring at and glared through the haze of rain at his friends marching ahead. He stopped in his tracks and said, "Hey fellas, there's something I've gotta do."

#

At last, C.D. reached the peak of the incline where the cliff-face plateaued. Boosting himself off a protruding root, he threw his right leg over the ledge and rolled onto his back, coughing and gasping.

Flat earth. *Hallelujah.*

The trees looked down at him, unimpressed.

He had no idea where the Cleaver might be, where the children might have run to, or how he was supposed to track down anyone who had such an insurmountable head start. He'd decided the Cleaver was just as batshit crazy as he'd expected upon arriving at his house of horrors, so the absurd circumstance in which he now found himself should come as no surprise. The man in charge was irrational, and now so was C.D.'s situation. At this point, he saw little recourse but to go through the motions, make it appear like he'd put forth an earnest effort to do what the Cleaver had ordered, so that once they met back at the Expedition to relocate the bodies, maybe there would be no further arguments or delays.

Just keep up appearances. Then, get the hell out of here.

He crawled to his knees and labored to stand, each new step a fresh torture. C.D. felt like he'd twisted six ankles rather than just the two. He shuddered and rubbed his arms, his waterlogged sports coat and silk shirt useless but to keep cold water clinging to his skin.

Limping up the trail, he soon came upon an empty cooler and a discarded canteen, which he raided for every last drop of clean water.

Through a clearing in the leaves, the view from the mountainside opened into a vast panorama of rolling hilltops and swaying trees. Beneath the mesh of branches along the cliffside, he saw the black metal of the Expedition. With the force of the storm, the forest before him undulated like an emerald sea. Only a distant roadway spoiled the illusion that he was standing in some exotic location. On any other day the view would be awe-inspiring, but today the sky roiled with dirty gray waves, and C.D. looked away.

That's when he saw the rope. A nylon rope had been wrapped and knotted around a tree trunk. C.D. followed the line as it angled upward to a thick branch alongside the trail. The rope draped the limb, and from it hung a small body swaying in the breeze several feet off the ground. A baseball hat concealed the child's face.

Thunder rolled.

Chapter 17 – Stormy Weather

"That's the dumbest thing I've ever heard," Clarence said, after Trainwreck announced his plan to head back the other way.

Joey agreed with Clarence. Trainwreck was crazy.

"It ain't dumb," Trainwreck said as he knuckled grime from his eyes while facing the other three in the middle of the trail. "I've got a plan and I've got an edge."

Joey noticed that even when soaked with mud, Trainwreck's ever-present cowlicks persevered, bobbing atop his head in total defiance of the storm.

"An edge?" Clarence said. "They've got guns!"

"Yeah, they *do*, don't they?" Trainwreck said in a serrated way that was more like making a statement. "At least, one of 'em does… I saw the skinny one scaling the far side of the ledge like he planned to come up behind us along the path. I saw him preenin' around in his city loafers and fancy clothes. He's just a lackey doing what he's told, and he's got no *grit*. And while we know he's coming, he won't know that I'm coming for *him*. That's my edge."

The Bobcats looked at each other covered with mud through a curtain of rain. Joey realized they appeared nearly interchangeable, their world now the color of coal and ash. He couldn't read his friends' expressions very well, but he was fairly certain Trainwreck wore a stone-cold grimace forged of steel that meant his decision had been made and there would be no point in further discussion.

"Your *edge*?" Paul said. "Train, don't pull this crap. It's insane."

"Yeah?" Trainwreck spat on the ground. "I guess that's what you get from a loose cannon."

"We need to stay together," Joey said. "We can't be far from the bridge."

"The bridge is just more running," Trainwreck said. "I'm done running. And I'm not going to argue 'cause I've made up my mind."

He turned and hiked back in the direction they had come.

"Don't go, man!" Clarence said as he watched him leave. "Trainwreck! *Zack!*"

"This is the worst idea ever," Paul muttered.

Joey knew it was useless to protest.

Once Trainwreck got about fifteen feet away, he turned back to the Bobcats. Clutching his fist with his other hand, he stared into the eyes of each of his friends for a long, sober moment. He then raised two fingers to his brow and chopped them down in a sharp, quick salute. "I love you guys. I'll see you fellas soon."

Then he walked away.

#

The rain grew fierce, and cold wind clawed through Trainwreck like a root grapple. As he made his return across the muddy mountain ridge, he tried not to think of himself as a gnat crawling along the backbone of an enormous angry god. He tried to block from his mind the many ways his plan could go wrong, and how any such mistake could put him in his grave. He tried to focus instead on any other distraction, such as the pelting rain that came and went in waves.

I need an umbrella.

He chuckled to himself and felt a little relief. His Gramps would've said it was raining "like a cow pissing on a flat rock."

He needed the levity. Needed any diversion from the hungry dogs of fear and doubt that barked and nipped at him with every step, just like they did on his walks home from school. He'd lost his MP3 player somewhere along the trail, so, to drown out the dogs he replayed in his head songs he knew from the radio. Fist-pumping songs that got the blood flowing, the kind that got a guy psyched up for a workout, a competition…or combat. Those sacks of crap who murdered Davey would soon find out Trainwreck was a "Street Fighting Man" like the Stones sang about. He's a guy who "won't back down," just like Tom Petty.

With those backbeats thumping in his head and his heart, he plotted the details of his ambush. He'd noticed a live oak along the trail a few minutes ago, and the idea had occurred to him instantly. Its trunk split into a Y about five feet off the ground. The trunk was *bifurcated*—a word he'd learned from Mr. Kilgore. Trainwreck could climb a prong of the fork to one of the thick branches that stretched over a small clearing in the trail. The clearing opened beyond a limestone hillside that obscured the tree from any hikers until they reached the hilltop. At that point, they'd be standing right beneath the big tree limb where

Trainwreck planned to be crouching in wait.

Hell from above, he thought to himself.

He hiked back past the oak to surveil the path around the hill for any sign of trouble. At the bottom where the ground leveled and widened alongside the foot of a tall pine, he saw a pale flash in the distance. His breath caught, and he leapt behind the trunk.

Another peek down the hazy trail—a fairly straight shot for nearly a hundred yards—confirmed the city-slicker gunman, wearing a tan coat and light-colored shirt, was limping up the path. Judging by the man's wavering gait, he didn't look very spry.

No grit, Trainwreck assured himself.

The big confrontation would arrive much quicker than he'd anticipated. Trainwreck dashed to the oak to get ready.

#

C.D. lumbered down the trail in a daze, shuddering from a merciless cold spell that bit to the bone. He knew the icy rot he felt inside came not only from the weather but from deep within him. It had gripped him the moment he'd laid eyes on the kid dangling from the tree. He'd recognized the boy's hat—Atlanta Braves, C.D.'s favorite baseball team. C.D. had worn a cap exactly like it as a youngster.

The Cleaver made me do it, he thought.

He felt like the wormiest maggot ever to wear leather shoes, because he was a grown-ass man, and he'd been the one to pull the trigger, to fire the shot that snatched away the boy's life. If he'd had any real guts when the big man had advanced on him, C.D. would have pointed the gun right between the Cleaver's eyes and blown the motherfucker's brains out.

But C.D. didn't have any guts.

Now he was a child killer.

A killer who was out of cigarettes.

I'd give a C-note for a cig, he thought. *A whole friggin' hundred.*

Lightning ripped a canyon high above the trees. Thunder quaked in its wake. Rain surged and pounded against C.D.'s wind-chilled flesh. The trail ahead broke uphill, and with each new step his ankles throbbed and his feet screamed at him in the dead language of broken blisters. He limped onward in true misery, and at that moment, he figured he probably deserved every bit of it.

#

The climb up the tree proved more taxing than Trainwreck expected. He hadn't accounted for the extra weight of the large stone he carried in his backpack. Even after dumping the other contents, the stone felt like a bowling ball belted to his back, dragging him down as he climbed.

But the rock had to be heavy. The rock was a bomb.

Now that he waited in position atop the thick oak limb, catching his breath despite a galloping heartbeat, the dogs had returned. The dogs of fear and doubt, yipping and snapping.

Ya can't pull it off, they seemed to say in barks and growls. *Ya just a kid. What exactly did ya have in mind, kid? Ya think you're going to kill him? Ya think ya could live with yourself if ya murdered somebody?*

Trainwreck once again let the drums kick in to drown out the dogs. Up in the tree, he stayed still and quiet, but on the radio station of his mind, the bass rumbled to life and the guitar howled.

I never said I was murdering anybody, Trainwreck thought. *Besides, you can't murder what ain't human. And that lowlife scum-sucker is less than human. Hell, he's less than animal. He murdered Davey in cold blood—murdered an unarmed kid—and if I don't do what I've got to do, then he's going to do the same thing to all the Bobcats. He'll track down Joey and Clarence and Paul and he'll pull that trigger three more times… If I get in his sights, then it will be four instead of three, and that ain't happening. All I'm doing is what I've got to do to defend my friends and everything the Bobcats stand for.*

And you know what?… I'm going to succeed.

The snap of the snare, the low-end thump of a floor-shaking beat, this was show time, so Trainwreck conjured up his favorite hard-rock songs and played them in his head like war drums. These songs quickened his pulse and steeled his nerves and tuned out the dogs and the downpour. They made him feel brave, even if deep down his self-doubt had eaten away his guts and left a great hollow. The songs filled that hollow with a fury, giving him a surge of sonic courage. These songs in his head, they got him ready.

Ready for whatever life throws at you, Joey would have said.

The thin man stumbled into view. He crept up the path with a careful slowness the way Trainwreck's grandma climbed a staircase, arms outstretched as if for balance. He wore a drenched pair of dark slacks that clung skin-tight, and although he still wore his city loafers, he nursed every step like he'd been tromping through thorns barefoot.

Trainwreck held his breath, frozen statue-still and dreading that the man might glance up at the tree limb. As he neared the strike zone below, Trainwreck spotted the pistol stuffed into the waistband at his back, above the right hip.

The sight of that gun pressed play on the next record. This was a special request. A battle song, and Trainwrecks's favorite. Cymbals crashed. He felt the bass guitar shake the ground and the electrical lead wail like a demon ghost. His heart thumped to a driving beat, and he tightened his ten-fingered hold on the football-size boulder he'd extracted from the mud alongside the trail.

With another limp, the murderer—*not human*—dragged his other leg behind him and stepped into the sweet spot below.

This was the moment Trainwreck had been waiting for. He pictured Davey flying backward as the explosion of gunshots echoed in his memory. Then he fixed his aim on the scalp of the murderer. The rock and roll raged within him.

If you want blood, he thought, *you got it.*

Trainwreck didn't just drop the rock. He slammed that

mother down.

#

Deadfalls. Stake pits. Tripwires. Snare traps…

Joey couldn't recount all the times the Bobcats had plotted the elaborate defense systems they would employ to defend HQ from enemy intruders. He and his friends had traded fantastical but plausible ideas about all manner of booby traps to waylay invaders approaching from the forest. The internet was a goldmine of dangerous guidance and instruction. Knowing an attack on their stronghold was imminent, they would have set up soup-can alarm systems around the perimeter, dug combat trenches, and stashed weapons caches at secret, nearby locations.

Joey's favorite idea had been Trainwreck's "feather spear trap," which he'd found on YouTube—a gnarly device made from tree limbs and vines. Trainwreck had even rigged up one with wooden spear tips he'd whittled with his survival knife. Spring-triggered by a tripwire, the trap would slice a tensioned branch through the air to stab prey with sharp daggers.

Things were different out here on Black Oak Mountain. The Bobcats were unprepared, on the run, and out of time to make a trap. And Joey was running low on ideas.

"What do we do after we cross the bridge?" Paul asked, pulling up beside Joey on the trail.

"I was hoping you had a plan," Joey said. "Got any dynamite? Too bad it's raining, or we could set it on fire and make it impassable. I don't know, maybe we could block it from the other side somehow…"

"That's all I can figure. Course, even if we figured out how to do that, it'd mean trapping Trainwreck on the other side."

Joey had already considered this. "Trainwreck's on his own. I don't want it to be that way, but *he* left. We can't wait around for him if there's a killer on our trail."

Paul didn't say anything, only dropped his pace and followed Joey, with Clarence right behind.

#

The rock glanced off the man's head. The stranger shouted and stumbled, pinwheeling his arms, but he did not fall. He had leaned away at the last crucial second, robbing Trainwreck of a direct hit with the boulder. Now the man clutched at his hair and staggered below.

Trainwreck pounced. Hooking an arm around the limb, he rolled off feet-first while swinging his legs ahead of him. Releasing the tree, he drop-kicked the man in the shoulders. Davey's killer left his feet with a grunt.

Trainwreck whapped onto the ground on his side. The impact jarred him, but he bounced right back up with a spike of adrenaline.

The man had smacked against a tree, bounced off, and spilled backward into the mud. Now he flipped over, moaned, and pushed himself up with one hand. With the other, he fumbled at his waistband for the gun.

Trainwreck gripped the survival knife strapped to his thigh and ripped it from its sheath. *Excalibur,* he thought.

What ya gonna do with that? barked the dogs.

Trainwreck drew back the blade. *I'll show you.*

The man's fingers pinched the pistol. Still on his knees, face blurred by rain and mud, he managed to pull it free. He brought it around to his front in an awkward grip while trying to stand.

Trainwreck lunged at him. Halving the distance between him and the gunman in a single stride. He brought the knife around in a wide swipe. The steel point stabbed hilt-deep into the man's forearm, and he screamed.

Trainwreck threw his shoulder into him, driving him backward off his heels. They both tumbled to the dirt. The man cursed and thrashed, but Trainwreck leapt astride him, wiry and determined. He grappled for the gun and managed to bat it out of reach. Trainwreck then went for the knife. Wrestling on the ground together, they each had a hand on the haft, but the pressure on the blade lodged in the stranger's arm made him howl.

Trainwreck rolled off him and took a new tact, scrambling for the gun. He slipped in the mud and pounded down on his chin, chomping his tongue. Blood filled his mouth with a sharp sting. He belly-flopped ahead, arm stretched out for the pistol just a few feet ahead.

"You fucker!" the man bawled from behind him.

With another dive ahead, Trainwreck got a mouthful of mud but reached the gun. He wrapped his fist around the handle and spun around on his butt. From his seated position on the ground, he lifted the pistol with both hands. He aimed the barrel at the chest of the man who'd killed Davey and now stood at the edge of the Gauntlet with his knife buried in his arm.

"Don't do it, kid," the man told him. But he must have sensed Trainwreck's determination, because the man spun around and leapt off the trail into the forest.

Trainwreck fired but missed. The man was gone.

Trainwreck dashed over to the trail edge. Beyond the brush, the forest floor dropped into a steep slope down the mountain. Davey's killer was somersaulting down the incline, flopping like a ragdoll. He smashed against a tree trunk, came to a rest, and then almost comically resumed his head-over-heel descent, until he dropped over an embankment where Trainwreck lost sight of him.

Train pointed the gun down the mountain and fired twice. He didn't have a shot, and there was no way to actually hit the man at this point, but he wanted to send a message loud and clear: If the pencil-neck wasn't already dead, he'd get that way real quick if he ever came around the Bobcats again.

#

The sound of the gunshots brought the Bobcats to a standstill. Joey swallowed a dry lump of nothing and turned to his friends behind him, who were likewise frozen in place. Wordlessly, they listened. The moment bled on.

Clarence appeared to shrink a couple of inches as he threw his hands to his face. Paul placed his fingers to his temples and stepped toward the forest, looking away into the trees, then down into the dirt.

Joey figured they pictured the same thing he did. The first shot had wounded Trainwreck from a distance, the other two had been fired at point-blank range.

Joey's heart felt constricted, and he pictured a mass of clutching black tendrils wrapping around it and squeezing ever tighter.

"How far away did those shots sound to you?"

Clarence's question stunned Joey, because it implied such a grim certainty about what had just unfolded that it need not be addressed, suggesting they best move on to more pressing matters.

It took Joey a moment to process. "I don't know," he said with a shake of his head. With all the noise of the wind and rain, sounds got confused, and he hadn't the skill to gauge by ear how far off the threat might be. Although, he had a hunch.

Paul said it for him. "It sounded closer than when Davey got shot, like they're following us up the trail, just what Trainwreck said they'd do."

Part of Joey felt he should say something about Train, some sort of eulogy or makeshift words of remembrance, but to do so would be to recognize a terrible truth they all seemed to want to avoid. Maybe they were right to keep their eye on escaping, at least for the time being. If they gave in to despair, they might never get out of it.

"Let's keep going," Joey said.

With heads down, the Bobcats pressed onward.

Chapter 18 – Thunderstruck

Trainwreck had done it.

Holy smokes, his plan had worked.

And to top it off, he didn't even have to shoot the guy! That big chicken had flown the coop as soon as the tables had turned! *No grit!* One look down the gun barrel and he'd taken a flying leap off the side of the mountain—*Jeez Louise!*

Trainwreck stared in drunken disbelief at the pistol. With rain running down his face and blood on his chin, he tried to collect himself and formulate a new plan. His head swirled with emotions—excitement, exhaustion, relief and terror, all tinged with the thrill of victory. He'd never imagined he would walk away from the encounter with the killer's gun in hand, yet here he stood, dizzy and free and alive. So very alive. He had so much nervous energy pulsing through him that his hands trembled. *Shaking like a dog poopin' peach seeds*, his Grandma would have said.

He checked the magazine, slid it back into the grip, and stuffed the 9mm into his waistband—the back not the front—so if it happened to discharge, it wouldn't shoot off his pecker.

He took a deep breath and cracked his knuckles. *Calm down. Get it together*, he thought. *Get your head on straight.*

Given that the whole event unfolded so quickly, Trainwreck figured if he beat his feet, he might catch the other fellas in short order, having halved their threat and armed the resistance.

At the foot of the live oak, he gathered his hidden waterlogged belongings, wrung them out, and returned them to his backpack. Not too much worse for wear, all things considered, even though his lip hurt like hell, and he was really going to miss his survival knife.

Trainwreck tightened his laces and cinched down his shoulder straps.

Suddenly, it occurred to him that the gunshots had alerted the second killer.

He broke into a steady jog back toward the bridge, stomping through the now-familiar mud and brambles of the Gauntlet. He could not wait to rejoin his friends.

He hadn't made it twenty yards when the woods came alive in front of him.

A tree left its roots and stepped into his path. Not a tree, but something nearly as big, covered in mud and leaves.

Shocked, Trainwreck halted, stumbling back. The tree took the form of a giant man-beast. Vines and leaves tangled the thing's hair like the swamp monster Trainwreck had seen in a Marvel comic. The figure's massive size and muscular bulk made it look like something from a movie, but what struck Trainwreck as very real were the triangular blades at the end of its arms.

Man-made weapons. Crudely welded. Two monstrous fists each gripping metal wedges the size of shark fins. Trainwreck had never seen anything like them.

The thing had to be human, and it stalked forward while drawing back one of those huge, steel fangs.

All the wind and rain seemed to go quiet, but Trainwreck's heart thundered. He felt the stolen gun in his grip, unsure how the pistol had gotten from his waistband back into his hand. He aimed it to fire, but the gun vanished, along with his hand. With a single swoop, the tree-man's blade had sliced through his arm.

Trainwreck's mouth fell agape as his hand landed on the ground, still gripping the pistol. The hand looked like rubber. Fake. Impossible. But the whiteness of bone on the stump of his wrist told no lies. Red ribbons wrapped snake-like down his forearm and ran thin with the water.

Trainwreck gasped in disbelief. He squeezed his elbow to stop the blood and tried to clench a fist that was no longer there.

The tree-man advanced. He drew back his other blade, high and near his head. On instinct, Trainwreck threw up his left arm to block it. The shark blade hacked straight through flesh and bone, and this time the pain seized him immediately.

Trainwreck groaned and fell to a knee. He raised his severed arms before him. Useless. The *nevers* swarmed him—never throw another ball, never hold a girl's hand, bait another hook, or give the secret handshake.

The dogs barked and snarled. *Told ya so! Told ya so!*

Tree-man took another step toward him as a deep black hole opened in the forest and beckoned Trainwreck into the void. But he wanted so badly to stay here, to see the fellas.

Lightning glinted off the raised blade.

Trainwreck thought, *Don't make it hurt.*

Then he fell into that deep black hole.

#

Paul rushed past Joey.

After descending a lengthy downhill bend, the trail leveled off and stretched before them in a straight shot through a tunnel of overarching pine limbs. Paul had been hiking a few feet behind when Joey heard him mutter something under his breath and quicken his pace, pulling beside him. Then Paul broke into a gallop, sprinting ahead with both his backpacks bouncing.

Joey glanced behind to see Clarence chugging up the rear but nobody else, nothing that might have frightened Paul, who was shrinking in the distance, maybe dashing for something he'd seen up the trail. Then his pace slowed. Joey watched him raise both arms and press them to his ears. Paul fell onto his knees and hung his head.

Joey broke into a run.

As he gained ground and the path forward came into clearer view, Joey saw the problem. His heart sank along with Paul's.

The Gauntlet had come to an end.

"You've got to be freakin' kidding me!" Clarence cried when he caught up.

It felt like a sick joke.

The trail ended at a steep ledge framed by two log-size metal pylons that once anchored Lonesome Bridge, but the bridge had broken. The now-tangled suspension cable and rotted deck boards draped down the jagged cliff-face like a broken promise.

Some two hundred feet below, a white-capped brown river raged with hunger.

The sight was shattering. For Joey, all hope seemed to bleed away like a candle burning with a cold, blue flame—his entire future melting out of form and running shapelessly down, down, down into that watery abyss.

Across the great divide, a similar sight taunted them. The remainder of the bridge, destroyed and decaying, hung down the opposite rock wall like an ugly stain. The thin air between here and there, maybe sixty yards as the bullet flies, seemed a vast and impossible distance.

On each side of the Bobcats, the forest twisted and twined together in a near-impenetrable morass, and the prospect of scaling down the cliff-face was a suicide mission.

They had reached a dead end.

Joey wanted his dad. He wanted to break down and wail like a toddler, to throw a helpless, fist-banging tantrum, then crawl into Dad's arms and let him make everything okay again. Let him fix the unfixable. Dad could fix anything, but he was gone. Although Joey didn't want the other fellas to see, the tears came in a rush. They flooded out of Joey hot and heavy and soul-shaking.

He covered his face and walked away—to where, he didn't care. He could hardly see but couldn't bear to face his friends, so he strolled back down the trail a ways.

"We're good as dead," Clarence said. "This is what they

mean in a comic book when someone says, 'we're doomed.' Because we're trapped now. This place is cursed. I *told* y'all!"

Maybe Clarence was right. Maybe Black Oak Mountain *was* cursed, and the Gauntlet was a trap that ate kids their age. Maybe they *were* doomed.

When Joey turned back around, Paul was leaning against a tree, holding a long, straight stick. He was whittling one end sharp with his pocketknife.

"What are you doing?" Joey asked him.

"I'm thinking."

Chapter 19 – The Big One

The Black Oak Mountain Ridge had long been a place of mystery, from its 1,300-foot peak to its bottomless valleys to its ancient black trees groping for sunlight like skeletal fingers. The forest hid secrets in its deadened lowlands and its slime-slicked lakes, where men could lose their way among leaf and limb and vine and darkness—even lose their sense of self. This land could be cruel and deadly, only meant for the birds, the bugs, the creatures of hoof and claw. Black Oak Mountain was the kingdom of predators like black vultures, timber rattlers, the beast in the cave, and the man known to others as the Cleaver.

For he knew the land and was one with the land, and now he stood large over his fresh kill—the child who felled the driver had proven easy to take down.

The Cleaver wiped off his blades and dropped them both into his canvas bag. They clanged against the metal inside. He tossed the boy's pistol into the bag, then grabbed the boy's ankles and dragged him off the trail. He draped him over a limb obscured in the shadows and left the body hanging, so he might retrieve it later and offer another prize to the cave.

Hoisting the duffel strap across his shoulder, the Cleaver turned back up the trail and gazed in the direction the others had fled.

The remaining young ones were searching for the bridge,

but that was no more. They would have no choice but to turn back the way they had come, and when they did, he would be there waiting for them. Despite the cold rain, his aches and pains, the tightness in his chest, and the creakiness of old bones, the Cleaver would wait as long as it took. He would never stop the hunt.

That's why the city folk like Heidecker would summon him to do their bloody deeds. They knew him to be as reliable as the sun and the moon. The Cleaver always won the hunt, year after year, corpse after corpse—a man who did not exist and could not be tracked, that never failed a mission. Partial to blades over bullets, his methods were quick and silent and baffling to everyone else.

Strange things happened sometimes. People disappeared with no explanation. He would come and go like a terrible dream, and in his wake, leave grief and mystery like calling cards.

The children had seen too much.

Now, the hunt was on.

#

With each Bobcat whittling intensely at their own stick, it didn't take long to fashion the crude weapons. They'd done enough thinking to carve three strong spears.

Joey remained acutely aware the killers carried guns. The lay of the land meant anyone coming down the trail would have ample time to squeeze off several rounds before he and his friends could take cover, much less strike with a spear. Still, after discovering the ruined bridge, Joey needed to keep his hands busy or he thought he might chew his nails to the bone.

"What's the plan?" Clarence asked, breaking the silence.

"Not many options," Joey said, honing a tip.

"I'll bet whoever is after us has known about the bridge all along," Paul said.

Clarence looked at the ledge and shook his head. "There's no way we can climb down there."

Joey stepped to the side of the path and examined the thick forest walls all knotted and raveled. The opposite side looked nearly as impenetrable. "Pitching off to the sides here will be like climbing through barbed wire. We'd first need to head back down the trail and find clearer ground. We don't want to get stuck in the briars and shot in the back."

"That pretty much settles it," Paul said. "Back the way we came."

"Right where the killers are at…" Clarence said.

"When we see the first opportunity, we ditch the trail," Joey said.

"Then we get lost in the woods…" Clarence closed his eyes and put a fist to his forehead.

Paul huffed air out of his nose and turned away from Clarence.

To change the subject, Joey pulled open his backpack and rifled through the contents. "Everybody check your stuff for anything we can use as a weapon."

"What's the point," Clarence muttered. "They've got guns. We don't."

"Shut up and do it!" Paul told him.

Clarence looked hurt, but he quit complaining.

Paul and Clarence checked their gear along with Joey, who found he hadn't packed anything more lethal than his short pocketknife. He'd be better off with the spear. While Clarence had made a good point—*why bring a spear to a gunfight?*—carrying any sort of weapon made Joey feel better than carrying no weapon at all.

Joey grabbed Davey's pack where it leaned against a tree. Inside, he found the official Bobcat handbook—Davey's unfinished project, which Joey now vowed to guard until his dying breath. Joey also found a compass, a digital camera, a first-aid kit, two maps, three pencils, a pair of binoculars, bug repellent, and *holy crap!*—

He envisioned Davey, bleeding on his back in the mud, staring up at his friends with only moments left to live. He'd tried to speak with his dying breath. Coughing and gasping, Davey had tried to tell them something he must have thought was damn important.

"*Take the buh…*" Davey had struggled to say.

"*The backpack?*" Paul had asked.

"*Take the buh…*"

"*The book?*" Joey had said.

Now Joey had a different hunch. Could Davey have been trying to tell them to "*Take the…BEAR SPRAY…*"?

From Davey's bag, Joey lifted up the silver canister of Bear-Away, labeled *Maximum strength compressed pepper spray repellent with a deployment range of 30 feet.*

"Hey y'all," Joey said. "Look what I found."

#

Thunder rippled along an eastward crack, but the rain slackened to a patter.

A fat toad, plump and peach-sized, hopped from the bushes onto the trail. It splashed into a puddle, skittered over to a rock, then leapt onto the black boot of the Cleaver. A swooping hand snatched the toad with thick fingers. The man opened his jaws wide and pushed the toad inside as it kicked and squirmed. He crunched the thing between his teeth, and it burst like a pocket of jelly. The man did not care for the taste of toad, always bitter from its fear-triggered urine, but it helped to fill the empty hole in his gut that yawned and gurgled—one of many nags from his treasonous body, eaten by age, eroded by toil, and now beleaguered by the footslog across the mountain, which had not been part of the plan.

The path was running short, however, and the terrain ahead teemed so thick with detritus that the forgotten trailway made the only passable route for travel. Because the woods thinned closer to his end, enabling a sideward descent off the mountain, he had to close the gap quickly between him and the children.

Otherwise, the rats could scramble away in all different directions.

It would not be long until they met. Now that the rain had thinned, the Cleaver had caught their scent. Fear tinged their stink with a sharp tartness that he knew well, and he could smell the children getting closer.

Chapter 20 – Plan B

Finding something was better than nothing, but Joey didn't place much faith in using a can of poison when facing a loaded gun. He found faith tough to muster these days. His dad had been better at that pursuit.

Joey remembered finding his dad kneeling at the foot of his bed one night soon after the diagnosis. His father's elbows had rested on the mattress with his hands cradling his head. Quietly, Joey had observed him from the doorway, having never seen him in such a state.

Joey's mother had already explained his dad's situation to him and that the prognosis was grim. Watching his father there by the bed, he felt so small, weak and powerless to help.

Eventually he said, "Dad? You okay?"

His dad had lifted up in a start. He then wiped his face, red and puffy, and smiled. "Hey, buddy. Yeah, I'm fine. Just saying a little prayer."

"A prayer?"

His dad had looked at him, and Joey saw something both solemn and earnest inside. "I should pray more. I do it mostly when I can't find the answers on my own. I don't want to trouble the Big Man Upstairs with my little problems, so I save the special requests for the major ones I can't figure out."

This had spoken volumes to Joey, because it told him the

man he knew as "the world's greatest fixer" didn't know how to fix all of the problems.

"You were asking God for help?" Joey had asked.

His dad nodded. "If anybody can give it to me, that's the guy."

Joey had thought on that for a moment. "Do you think God will answer your prayer?"

Again, his father nodded. "God always answers prayers but He works in mysterious ways. Sometimes the answer is *no*."

The idea that God would turn his back on his dad gave Joey a shudder.

"Dad," he'd said, trying to swallow the frog in his throat. "Are you scared?"

His father then tried to smile, but it quickly shrank to a thin, flat line. "Son, I'm not going to lie to you. I'm very scared. I'm terrified. But I want you to understand: It's not dying that I'm afraid of; it's losing you and your mom. I can't bear the thought. And not just for my own sake, but for yours—the feeling that I might not be around to watch you grow up, that I won't be there when you and your mom need me. It feels like a job I haven't completed, like I'm shirking my duty, and that's what I was asking God to give me…just a little more time with you guys."

Tears had brimmed in Joey's eyes, and he tried to force them back. "I didn't think you ever got scared of anything. You're the bravest man I know."

His dad had sat down on the bed and extended an arm for Joey to sit next to him, which he did. Dad hugged him, placed a hand on his shoulder, and said, "Son, everyone gets scared. I just try to hide it. All men try to hide it. Having courage doesn't mean you're never afraid. Having courage means you don't let the fear beat you. You don't let it get the best of you. You overcome it."

Joey had held him tight. "I love you, Dad."

"I love you too, Joey," his father had said.

Now, as the Bobcats marched back up the Gauntlet with spears at the ready, Joey said a silent prayer. He asked God to give them a whole lot of courage and a great deal of luck.

Paul took point.

Joey carried the bear repellent.

Clarence kept asking questions. "What if they open fire?"

"We've been over this," Paul told him.

"I just don't see how it will work."

"It might *not* work," Paul said. "I'm open to other suggestions."

Clarence dropped his head.

The final plan they'd discussed was to flee down the side of the mountain as soon as the landscape thinned. Take their chances with a compass, rather than a gunman. The woods flanking the trail remained impassable, however, and would not thin until they crested the hill they now climbed.

Everyone understood Plan A, but Clarence had questions regarding Plan B: What to do if they encountered the gunmen while stuck on the trail. That plan was hazy.

Plan B had two options. Option one was to dash into the thicket and likely get shot in the back. Option two was Paul's idea; to charge the sons of bitches. He reckoned that would at least give them a fighting chance. If they got within range of the pepper spray, maybe they could blind their attackers and disable their aim. With three people charging, even if two got shot, the third might drive a spear through the hearts of the bad guys. Option one was a coward's death, while with option two, the Bobcats went down swinging.

They decided on option two. Once they accomplished that goal, escaping off the mountain would become top priority…escaping *together*.

"I want y'all to know that if anything happens, I won't leave you," Joey said. "I'll stick with you. I mean it. I swear on my dad's grave."

The other two let that sentiment lay for a moment.

"Same goes for me," Paul said. "I've got your backs, no matter what."

"Me too," Clarence said. "Bobcats forever."

The three maintained a steady gait along the trail with their spears at their hips.

"Keep your eyes on the woods," Paul said. "Someone might be hiding in the scrub for an ambush."

"Great," Clarence grumbled.

"Remember, if we have to fight, stay on your feet." Paul watched a lot of UFC matches on TV. "Don't try to kick or you might lose your footing and fall. If we all make it past them, then forget the fight. Our best bet is to haul butt down the trail and off this mountain."

"And don't hesitate," Joey said.

"Not for a second," Paul said. "If you've got to stab one of those suckers, you stab him. If you've got to punch them, then let 'em have it. Remember, when you throw a punch, lead with your middle knuckle. Do it with confidence. Picture yourself getting it right, then just act out the picture."

Clarence made a fist and practiced his form.

"And whatever you do…" Paul continued—but then he stopped mid-sentence.

Joey saw why Paul stopped talking.

Joey had learned some hard truths about life. That it comes at you fast. That you get no "time-outs" and your plans don't mean squat. He had learned that stone-cold killers walked among them.

As the Bobcats crested the hill to a flat stretch of trail, one such killer seemed to materialize out of the haze, standing silently in the middle of the Gauntlet, some thirty yards down the path. A living nightmare of outlandish proportions, the thing looked like some primitive throwback, a sasquatch or yeti, were it not for those boots and the huge army bag clutched beneath one massive arm.

The Bobcats froze. Joey's breath went still. His heart pounded like a mallet on meat. Somewhere to the west, the screech of a hawk marked the moment.

No one said a word.

Joey studied Davey's murderer…the *big one*, as Trainwreck had called him. Had he killed Trainwreck too? The height and bulk of the man had to be the result of a mutation, some hybrid half-creature sideshow freak who would have been caged or hunted in darker times. Under the circumstances, that would have been just fine with Joey, who fixed on his face with terrified focus, mesmerized. The man's eyes were hidden within a shroud of matted hair, and that was a relief, because Joey knew what he would see in those eyes. Darkness. Blackness. The wriggling tentacles of ink and crude, purging out of the sockets from an overflow of pure, vicious evil. The man who stood before them was a husk-maker, and Joey knew if he were to take even one look into those eyes, he would go stark, raving mad.

With his right arm, the beast-man reached into his bag and drew out a long, broad metal blade with two handles along an edge, one at the end and the other near the center. The steel looked at least four feet long, and the man gripped its handles with each palm and held it aloft. It was a great knife. A broadsword. An enormous machete that he would use to cut them to pieces.

The bag fell.

The man lurched forward.

"Guys?" It was Clarence.

"Get ready." That was Paul.

His friends' voices plinked around in Joey's mind without meaning. This was the end, and nothing had meaning. They were prey to be slaughtered by this ancient hunter, skinned for their hides and cooked into stew meat.

Soon, they would all be husks. Forgotten, unfound, bones rotting in the mud.

"Joey, you got the spray?" Paul said from his left.

"Oh god, I don't like this," Clarence whispered from Joey's right.

Joey stayed quiet—a statue frozen in time and space. The killer appeared to grow in amazing scale as he stalked forward. He moved with the unchallenged supremacy of a king in his castle.

"Joey, you still with us?" Paul asked.

Now twenty yards away, Joey got the foul stench of the man, the stink of rot and death and blood and feces. This is what Hell smelled like.

"Get that spray ready, Joey!" Clarence said.

Joey had the pepper spray stuffed into the rear pocket of his blue jeans, and that's where it stayed. He kept his hands on the spear, gripping so tightly that his fingers went numb.

Fifteen yards away, the stride of the beast-man gained speed. The *thud-thud-thud* of his boots splashed through the mud.

"Joey, snap out of it!" Paul said.

Joey didn't budge.

Closing fast, the man bared black teeth. He gave a low growl. The blade rose high.

"Screw this!" Clarence dropped his spear and twisted over to Joey, snatching the canister out of his pocket. He raised the can with both hands, thumbed off the safety, and aimed. "Eat this, motherfucker!"

He hit the trigger. Chubby ol' Clarence, who could never hit a baseball or ever sink a basket, nailed that big ugly bastard right between the mother and the fucker. A thick rope of liquid struck the beast-man square in the face, coating him with a searing chemical concoction that must have eaten right into his eyes and nostrils, judging by the way he roared.

Joey woke up.

Paul yelled, "*Charge!*" He and Joey dashed forward, spears first.

The killer swung his knife as Joey lunged forward. The blade broke Joey's spear and knocked it off course. Paul followed with his own, stabbing the man's thigh.

In a backhand swipe, the killer slung his weapon and caned Joey across the chest with the handle edge. Joey left his feet, smacked against a tree trunk, and slipped to the ground. He gasped for air but drew no breath.

Paul's spear ripped from his hands as the man twisted around. The killer snarled. With a sweep of his good leg, he kicked Paul's feet out from under him. Paul slammed to the ground. He flipped onto his back as the beast-man raised a huge knee and stomped a boot down onto his shin with a sickening crunch. Paul screamed.

The killer stepped across Paul and raised his giant cleaver to slay him.

"Get off him!" raged Clarence, who'd gathered his spear and came running full speed. The sharp wooden tip drilled through the air and plunged into the man's side, just above the hip. The killer seized up. His elbows buckled, and the blade he lofted clapped down against his chest.

Joey, back on his feet and gasping, grabbed his broken spear from the ground. His eyes watered and his throat burned from the lingering pepper mist.

Paul tried to stand. When he put weight on his leg, his shin folded beneath him. He shrieked. As he started to fall, Clarence scooped him beneath the shoulders and jerked him backward.

"Over here!" Joey shouted.

The beast-man whirled around at his voice and again raised the cleaver for the kill. Joey moved to his left, and the killer pivoted to follow him, standing between Joey and his friends.

Joey thrust his stick at the killer. A swat of the huge blade knocked it away like a toothpick.

Clarence seized the moment. With Paul on his shoulder, he leapt down the path with stunning agility.

The killer spun around to grab them but staggered from the two spears protruding from his body. That's when Joey dashed behind him. They'd all made it past!

Joey and Clarence each lifted Paul beneath an arm and hauled him down the path in a panic.

With a quick glance back, Joey saw the killer pull the spear from his side and cast it away. Clarence stared straight ahead, huffing and puffing, eyes red from the spray cloud. Paul's face twisted in agony. Joey looked back once more and saw the beast-man receding as they ran, but now the other spear was out of his leg. Staring down the Gauntlet at the Bobcats, the killer held the whittled branch before him in two huge fists and snapped it in half.

Joey turned away. "Let's get off this mountain. Fast!"

Chapter 21 – Damaged

The trill of her ringtone startled Janice Kilgore, who sat on the sofa transfixed by the weather report on TV. Conditions looked grim on Black Oak Mountain.

Her display screen showed a number she didn't recognize, but with a local prefix, so she gambled it was no telemarketer and answered.

"Hello."

"Hello, this is Juanita Barkley, Clarence's mother. I'd like to speak to him, please."

"I'm sorry, Clarence isn't here right now," Janice said. "I believe he's camping with the other boys."

"Excuse me? Camping?"

"Yes…" Janice spoke cautiously, "It was my understanding they had all gotten their parents' permission."

"No. This is the first I've heard of any camping. Camping where?"

"I dropped them off yesterday at Black Oak Mountain."

"Oh my god."

Janice swallowed. "Joey and three other boys are with him. I'm sorry. They assured me that—"

"Where did you drop them off exactly?"

Janice eyed the weather map while a handsome meteorologist gestured to a massive bank of digital red blobs that approached the mountain in incremental flashes. Another wave of thunderheads would soon pummel her son and his friends.

"The trailhead on Shady Grove, where all the sports vehicles enter the woods. I'm supposed to meet them tomorrow at the Oak Hill soccer fields."

"Have you heard from them since?"

"No. Joey doesn't carry a phone. My understanding is that the reception drops off out there."

"Oh my lord, my heart is pounding ninety to nothing."

"I never expected the weather to get this bad or I would have put my foot down."

"I have to go, Mrs. Kilgore," said Juanita, now curt and frosty. "If you hear from them, will you please give me a call? You have my number."

"Yes, of course. Absolutely."

Juanita hung up, and Janice sat there listening to the dead line for a while. She imagined herself sprouting donkey ears like the kids in Disney's *Pinnocchio*, and expected the other parents would soon picture her the same way.

#

After a close look at Paul's leg, Joey felt woozy. He palmed the ground to steady himself and stared up at the sky, searching for a calming cool blue and finding only roiling, dirty gray. The sight of blood had never made him swoon, but exposed bone was another story. After cutting away Paul's pants leg despite all his grunting and gnashing, Joey and Clarence found both his calf bones not only broken but shattered, with white shards tearing through the skin.

"How bad is it?" Paul gasped.

"It's reeeally broken," Clarence said. "Like *bad*."

"Oh jeez…" Paul writhed on the ground and clenched his teeth. "Crap, it hurts so bad!"

"It's a compound fracture. We've got to get you to a hospital," Joey told him, catching his breath. Mr. All-American's days on the baseball field were over for now and maybe forever, and this tugged Joey's heart right down into the mud, realizing his friend's dreams for a scholarship out of Trapper Valley had been smashed to pieces along with his leg. He'd never seen Paul vulnerable.

Joey turned to Clarence. "We need a stretcher."

Clarence nodded. "Yeah…*yeah*…like Davey showed us." His voice lifted with a note of recognition. "I'll find a couple good branches."

After they'd loped down the trail until the killer was far out of sight, with Paul hopping between them, everyone had collapsed to the ground to regroup. They'd been running for twenty minutes.

"What about…" Paul stammered. "What about…the other guy that Train saw?"

"I don't know," Joey said.

Nobody had an answer, and they were all too shaken to

conversate. Joey searched for sticks to make a splint, and Clarence scrambled to cobble together a stretcher, just like they'd practiced during one of Davey's battlefield triage exercises. Rifling through the backpacks, he came up with a zippered windbreaker and one of Paul's spare hoodie sweatshirts. They inverted the sleeves of each garment, stuffing the arms inside the jackets and down along the sides. With the clothes lying on the ground end to end, Joey and Clarence threaded two stripped-branch poles lengthwise through the sleeves as lateral supports for a makeshift stretcher.

All the while, Joey kept his head on a swivel, glassing the woods for the skinny gunman or the hairy giant who had survived their spears and snapped them like twigs.

While lifting Paul onto the stretcher, Joey tried to touch only the splint and not his friend. Paul moaned anyway, and Joey wanted to vomit.

At last, they got him settled and each took two handles, with Joey at the front and Clarence at the other end near Paul's head. They heaved him upward, and he groaned as the jackets folded, wrapping him like a taco.

"Put him down, put him down!" Clarence said. "We forgot the crossbars."

"Right, sorry." Joey helped lower Paul back down, where he gave a sigh of relief.

"I'll handle it," Clarence said. "You go be our lookout."

Joey nodded to Clarence and faced back down the trail. In the melee, Clarence had dropped the bear spray, or what was left of it. Their spears were gone too, and they had no time to make new ones. With nothing left but a pocketknife, Joey felt naked.

Still, he jogged back up the trail through the dense gray woods, exposed and unnerved by the eerie sensation of countless eyes watching his every move. The killer was nowhere to be seen, but the beast-man was everywhere and anywhere, chameleon-like in his mud-caked camouflage. That was his superpower, and Joey saw his phantom image in each stretch of shadow and etched into the bark of every tree.

Joey crept up the trail dreading that the beast-man's huge, groping hand might rip right out of the ground and snatch his ankle. He might emerge from the foliage like a gator from a swamp. Nothing seemed beyond the limits as the day grew long, the eastern sky dimmed, and Joey felt smaller and smaller.

Although he saw no sign of trouble, the hairs on his neck stood stiff as bristles. He stopped his jog, took a deep breath, and said, "Heck with this."

By the time, he returned to his friends, Clarence was completing the final lash on two short, wooden crossbars he'd attached at each end of the stretcher to keep it square and give it rigidity.

Their second attempt at lifting Paul succeeded, and they slogged on down the Gauntlet with him laid out between them. The three boys had hobbled past their friend's body, where it hung limp and out of sight in a tree.

The Cleaver returned to that spot, still squinting and sneezing, chest heaving, laboring from a gash in his side and the deep hole above his knee. The face full of poison had been a new and instructive experience — a weapon he'd not expected so deep in the forest, one more associated with city women who carried purses. Its effect impressed him with an onslaught of all senses, arresting his breath, rendering blindness, driving an acrid, wet fire into his pores.

Although his vision remained blurry, he located the dead boy's backpack where it leaned against the tree. Finding a downed log on which to rest, the man snatched open the pouch and took out a canteen. The water rinsed his eyes and bathed his salt-dry tongue. Beneath a razor-keen blade he'd long ago forged from a foot of scrap iron, the wet denim on his thigh parted to reveal a rugged red hole as big around as his finger. At the slightest touch of the blade tip, the wound stung like a hornet. He took another mouthful of water, then spat a stream into his injury to wash out the dirt. Seeing too little blood to indicate anything but a flesh wound, he ripped away the hanging boy's shirt and wrapped the cloth around his thigh, cinching it tight.

Now to clean his wounded side, and then he'd resume the hunt with a vengeance.

Chapter 22 – The Hungry Mountain

C.D. woke shrieking as a cocoon of pain sank its teeth into him. Nails… Huge, metal nails like the spikes that anchor railroad ties… Dozens of those nails—maybe hundreds—must have been staked into C.D.'s flesh from all angles. That could be the only answer, he thought in a bleary haze. His racking agony defied his skeletal paralysis like some merciless cosmic punishment. He could barely move a muscle, but could feel everything, helpless but to lay there and suffer.

He could twitch his knee a little, so maybe his spine was intact, but his legs were torn and twisted. It seemed blood or mud had caked one eye closed, and the other opened only to dark shadow. His arm, if still attached, must lay somewhere behind his head, but his shoulder refused to retrieve it. Each time he shifted his torso, those rail spikes dug in and twisted.

Where the hell was he, anyway? And how did he get here?

Judging from the feel of solid rock on each side of his face, he figured he must have fallen into some sort of crevice, a man-sized crack between two massive rock walls. The wind and rain meant he was outdoors, and gradually the memories of the forest became clearer. Black Oak Mountain. Heidecker. The blue and red Braves hat. The dead boy. The Cleaver…

It all came back in a rising tide. The crazy kid from the tree. Losing his gun. The shattering fall down the rocky incline.

Realizing he'd seen a multitude of limestone projections riddling the mountainside, the idea that he'd become wedged down into one seemed ever more likely. C.D. was stranded out here in the forest at night with a broken body and waning hope. As these truths became evident, C.D. parted his lips to scream, but only managed a weakened moan the wind swallowed up and forgot.

#

"It's getting dark fast," Clarence said between huffs and puffs.

"Still got a while before nightfall," Joey replied. "It's the cloud cover that's killing the light."

Paul's stretcher got heavy fast. Joey's adrenaline waned, and he could tell Clarence was winding down too. Having trampled the trail on the way up was a help on the way back, but carrying Paul between them had erased any advantage that would have hastened their travel. Each time they hit an incline, they had to slow to a crawl and inch down the slope with the stretcher. Twice they had tipped it and dumped Paul into the mud. Even on straightaways, the weight of the burden seemed to steadily increase, and Joey's fingers had gone numb beneath the pressure.

Progress was grueling, but the Joey and Clarence soldiered onward. It's what Joey's dad would have done. It's what any Bobcat would do.

#

The wounded leg refused to obey.

The Cleaver had become accustomed to pain as if it were his own long shadow, a dark companion which would never leave. Old bones. Dirty lungs. Rotten guts. These things made his dull aches and shooting pangs a common occurrence, like an infestation of mysterious vermin gnawing him from the inside out. Pain was a nuisance, but one he could overcome.

More difficult to control was his body's refusal to comply with orders, like with that treacherous leg. After the injury, it no longer wanted to bend right. The gash in his side directly above it only exacerbated the problem; his hip did not shift correctly on command of his brain. The shell of meat he wore had deteriorated and was turning against him.

A total betrayal by his physical form, the Cleaver of late found himself trapped in his body and cursed by age, and this curse had been impacting his work. His strength was off. His reflexes had slowed. His lungs would slow their function at critical moments. When faced with a challenge, the Cleaver knew to crush it, to cut through any obstacle like a scythe through a stalk. Now, facing an enemy within, he found his hands bound, powerless to fight.

This was mutiny.

He would not relent, though, because he had a job to do. Retreat was a foreign concept and success a foregone conclusion. He would override his double-crossing body, full steam ahead.

He would strip the gears, throw a rod, and burn up the engine if that's what it took.

So, he lumbered back down the path tracking his game, treating the stubborn leg like a dead prop and growing ever more furious with his flesh, and with the three young boys whom he intended to slay. He could practically taste the kill.

He could definitely smell them.

#

"Any signal yet?"

Clarence held his phone up to the cloudy sky. He walked in a circle then lowered his arm. "No."

They had stopped alongside the trail to rest. Joey sat on the ground with his back against a tree trunk, trying to collect water in his canteen from a dribbling leaf. After taking stock of his pain and exhaustion, he decided the only part of him that didn't hurt was his hair.

Clarence sat down on the ground and stretched out onto his back with a sigh. "I might not ever be able to stand again."

Paul lay on the stretcher, shivering in his sleep. His clothes were drenched, as were all their belongings, and Joey couldn't think of an effective way to keep him warm without building a fire. They had been hiking for hours with no sign of the killers, but that was no comfort to Joey. It only meant the killers held the element of surprise, and he refused to stay put in one place until he and his friends made it back to civilization.

But taking a moment to rest was something he simply could

not do without.

Dusk had gathered the gloom around them. Shadows were blending together like blooms of ink, morphing the forest into an impenetrable mass of black.

"How are we on flashlights?" Clarence asked, as if reading Joey's mind.

Joey capped his canteen and rummaged through his backpack, retrieving the ten-inch Maglite his dad had given him for Christmas. "Got mine."

Clarence clicked on a fluorescent light the size of a pill bottle, then clicked it off. "We'll use mine as a backup. Yours throws more light."

"Okay with me." Joey coughed. His voice had gone weak and raspy.

Clarence took a sip from his canteen. "Paul, you awake?"

When Paul didn't answer, Clarence crawled over to him and nudged his shoulder. "How you doing, buddy?"

Paul groaned.

Clarence tilted his canteen and poured a thin stream of water onto his friend's lips. He placed his palm to Paul's forehead. "I think he has a fever."

Joey had suspected as much, but hearing it spoken made it a grim reality. He knew the possibility of infection from an open wound, especially out here in the mud and the wild. Time was working against them harder than ever.

Clarence climbed to his feet. "We need to get a move on."

Joey closed his eyes and winced but knew his friend was right.

#

C.D. awoke again to a strange intuition that something dangerous lurked nearby. Maybe he had heard a noise while unconscious, or perhaps, he thought, smelled a particular pheromone that triggered some latent survival instinct. He had learned about such natural reactions in high school biology, a class he'd always enjoyed even when pretending to be too cool to give a shit. On opening his one good eye, he saw the darkness of his predicament had grown even blacker, indicating the sun had set; dinnertime for any nocturnal hunters on the prowl.

And here he lay, buffet style.

The forest swished and pattered with wind and rain. To detect any other noise within the stormy susurration took keen attention and a discerning focus, but C.D. thought he heard the crunch of a footfall on twigs. If only the storm would quiet, but it stubbornly blew harder and splashed rain against the rock that trapped him.

Again, he tried to move his arm. Nothing. His legs…only a wiggle. He'd wet himself earlier, and again the urge to urinate gripped his bladder and squeezed.

He listened. Was that another crunch?

That asshole Vinnie the Cat…this is all his fault.

At that instant, if C.D. had had two magic wishes, the second would be to see that fucker duct-taped and covered in gasoline as someone struck a match and set him afire.

The pop of a broken branch told him something large was afoot. He felt a presence nearby, like a slight change in pressure from the displacement of air. Then came a huff that could only be the breath of an animal.

C.D.'s bladder released. The warmth spread over his crotch.

He knew the smell of blood tantalized carnivorous predators, and he need not see his injuries to expect a lot of open wounds, red and glistening, mouthwatering.

The thing moved with heavy noise through the brush around his location, crushing whatever lay in its path. The noise came from below, as though something were pacing at the base of the rock mass where he lay immobilized. It brought with it a feral smell of old meat and manure.

On hearing a scraping sound, C.D. pictured sharp claws scratching against stone, trying to find a grip so the beast could climb up and kill.

The thing below gave a low, rumbling growl, and C.D. gave a whimper. The creature was on the move again. C.D. followed its grumble from the direction of his head around toward his left. Despite his disorientation, C.D. had an inkling that the creature was ascending the hillside. If it had caught his scent, it soon would be approaching him from above, and not below.

Thunder crashed, and he caught flashes at his periphery.

Oh, what he wouldn't give to be back in Birmingham, snuggled up in *Sin-Dee's* warm bed and puffing on a post-coital cigarette.

From the direction of his feet, the growls grew louder. C.D.'s heart beat faster. The scratching noises meant the claws had found stone and now walked upon it. Bass-heavy breathing huffed from what must be barrel-sized lungs. C.D.'s mind reeled with images of monstrous wolves, giant cougars, and hungry bears.

He found he could move, but only by trembling. The creature closed in on him from behind, its growl gigantic over his squeak-like whimper.

Claws raked down his back and hooked his waistband. C.D. was heaved out of the crevice, screaming. Sliding backward, his faced dragged against rock as his body slung around lengthwise. His head thumped on soft ground.

Something huge hovered over him, straddling his chest. Its hot breath passed over his nose, the smell rancid and wild. C.D. tried to scamper backward, but only one leg kicked and it found no leverage or grip.

Beneath the bright white of a lightning strike, the thing reared back, and C.D. saw it. Both eyes gleamed like black pearls. It stood taller than man and as broad as a bear, but hairless with gray and rippled skin. With pointed ears and a long snout, its jaws opened wide and brandished flesh-ripping fangs to back its blood-curdling roar—the most terrifying sound C.D. had ever heard.

Its head thrust down and bit into his ribs with a crunch. C.D. howled like a beast himself until he could do it no more. Then he gasped and gagged as the creature ate him alive.

#

Somewhere in the woods, the Cleaver heard the distant wail of a familiar voice, and he understood. Heidecker's driver was dead now. The beast would eat well tonight. He took solace in that which nourished the beast, for it was a kindred spirit, and also an exalted one, a fellow traveler of purer breed and nobler pursuit. A creature to be admired. A god to be worshipped.

Long live the beast.

Now for the children.

Chapter 23 – Darkness Descends

The rain returned in a downpour. Joey was so wet, he figured even his bones must be soggy. For what seemed an eternity, he and Clarence had slogged through the forest driven by a mission, but now their progress slowed to a crawl. Joey's legs ached, his shoulders throbbed, and his fingers barely had the strength to grip the stretcher. The ground was slick, and he could hardly see a thing with the flashlight he had tied to the stretcher handle. Every root tried to trip him while the surrounding branches lashed at his face and limbs. He snatched gasps of air like a drowning victim.

Then the ground gave way.

A sudden mudslide rushed down the mountain and swept his feet from beneath him. He lost hold of the stretcher and slid off the trail. Paul's gurney crashed to the ground. Clarence shouted from behind him. Joey slammed onto his side and went skidding down the hillside into darkness, caught in some sort of water-carved gulley. Rocks pounded and tore at him. Helpless but to spin along and ride it out, he feared he would soon hit a dead tree and be impaled by a limb. Eventually, he spilled over a bank and came to a halt on level ground.

With a splash from behind, something else landed in the shallows after him. Joey recognized Clarence's grumbling voice.

Joey caught his breath and said, "You okay?"

From somewhere in the pitch black ahead of him, Clarence coughed. "I think I'll live."

"Where's Paul?"

"A little further up the slope," Clarence said. "I think I rolled over him."

"Can't see anything out here," Joey said. Shielded from starlight by the forest canopy and now without a flashlight, the overwhelming darkness of the woods settled over them like an endless black blanket. He whipped his arms out to fling off the mud.

He heard Clarence rummaging around.

"Good thing we got this," his friend said as he clicked on the penlight from his pack.

They hiked back up the slope to find Paul had spilled off the stretcher and lay unconscious a few feet away from it. The stretcher appeared intact, but the flashlight was missing, and the idea that Paul had slept through the whole ordeal gave Joey a grim feeling. How could anyone ride the Indiana Jones Express down the mountain and sleep through it all...unless they were already half dead?

As Paul slept, at least he was unaware of any new pain. Joey now hurt in fresh places he had not thought possible, as though someone had taken a salad fork and stabbed him with random perforations from head to toe.

"How far off the trail do you think we are?" Clarence asked.

Having lost all sense of direction and now blind, Joey shrugged. "No idea."

After securing Paul back on the stretcher and moving him to

flat earth, they covered him with spare clothes from their sparse packs to warm him as best they could. The wet clothes wouldn't do much but trap what little body heat he could generate, but the only belongings they'd managed to keep dry were the Bobcat manual and Paul's framed photo of Candace Worton—both protected by flimsy plastic grocery bags.

Joey and Clarence huddled around Paul and thought for a while. In the soft glow of the penlight, their friend looked pale and weak.

"Maybe we should stay put," Clarence said.

"I'm not sure we got a choice." Joey didn't know which way to go, and to head in the wrong direction could be disastrous. Their compass pointed the way north—the general direction back to Trapper Valley—but due north meant home lay on the far side of the mountain.

Clarence investigated their surroundings with the pen-light, circling Joey and Paul like a single firefly in infinite space. Halfway around the site, Joey heard a small splash.

"There's water over here," Clarence called. "You think it might be that lake we walked around?"

"Could be. Or it could be any other creek or pond along the range."

"If it's *that* lake, then we aren't far from the trailhead."

"You get a phone signal yet?" Joey asked.

"No. Battery is about to die, too."

"Of course it is…"

Clarence came back and settled next to Paul and Joey beneath a tree trunk. "Think we should lay low?"

"Just until first light so we can see where we're going," Joey said. "Last thing we need is to end up washed into a lake. We couldn't even stay on the trail."

Clarence clicked off his pen-light. "Guess there's no point in advertising our location."

The sudden blackness swallowed them like the mouth of a whale. Joey was stunned by the total absence of visibility out here miles from artificial light and beneath the midnight cloud cover that snuffed the moon and heavens. He'd never experienced such pure and total darkness.

"I'll take first watch," Clarence said.

That was fine, Joey thought. *That way we'll have two of us on guard duty, 'cause there's no way I can sleep out here with a killer on the loose…maybe two of them.*

Joey laid beneath the tree, scared witless and utterly exhausted. The hiss and patter of falling rain confused all sense of sound, and every odd little racket put him on edge. Every thump was the stomp of the beast-man. Each rustle was a woodland creature scurrying out of the killer's path. Joey's imagination seemed to take glee in the games it played. He imagined he heard the heartless cackle of that witch, Mother Nature. He felt the tickle and twitch of her minions on his skin; things that crawl, things that slither, things that fly around at night. He kept reminding himself it was all in his mind. At least, most of it.

If only Dad were here. Or, if he were home with Mom. Oh, how

Joey wanted a warm hug from Mom.

Noises, this way and that. He dared not keep his eyes peeled… at least, he tried his best. He would stare hard in the direction of each new sound and see utterly nothing. Were his eyes even open? Blinking, he could see no change, no difference in contrast or color. Darkness reigned with his eyes open or closed, and Joey began to doubt himself. He began to doubt his consciousness and in turn, his sanity. Was he awake or asleep? Could this present state be a dream?

Had the whole damn trip been a nightmare?

These thoughts stormed and crashed along with the weather as Joey shivered on the ground in a quiet, fretful fit, wrestling with his very mind.

Eventually, all went still, and everything went silent.

#

Screams shattered the silence.

Joey blinked awake to the silver light of breaking dawn, realizing it was Paul's voice shrieking in terror. The woods rustled and crunched with commotion just a few feet away.

"Stop it! Help!" Paul shouted. "*Hellllp meeee!*"

Joey shot upright, and his eyes adjusted to his friend's anguished face upside-down and screaming as he slid away from him along the forest floor. Dragging Paul was the monstrous beast-man, hauling him by the ankles while twisting his friend's ruined leg like a rag.

Paul tore at the ground to anchor himself, grabbing stones

and weeds which would unearth in his grip. Clawing and thrashing, he slid along helpless, until the killer neared the thick trunk of a tall pine. Clutching Paul's ankles together in both hands, the man squared his huge legs in line with the tree and wrenched his wrists, flipping Paul onto his belly.

"Let go of him!" Joey shouted. Delirious. Disoriented with a sudden rush of panic, he scrambled to his feet, stumbling.

"Don't! No don't it!" Paul howled.

The killer reared back, twisted his torso, and threw his weight to one leg. In a wide swath, he whipped Paul's body through the air like a baseball bat. The back of Paul's head smashed against the tree trunk. A spray of blood fanned outward in a halo. When Paul dropped to the ground with one eye bulging, Joey knew it was over.

"Noooooooo!" bellowed Clarence at his left. Joey saw him fall back against a tree and clutch at his mouth.

The beast-man dropped Paul's ankles. He spilled forward from momentum onto his wounded thigh and snatched a nearby sapling to steady himself. With a drooping head and heaving shoulders, he turned to face Joey.

Paul's death had shattered something inside Joey. At the sight of it, his mind overloaded, and he felt a break the instant Paul's skull hit the pine—a mental noise like an explosion of stained glass. It all became too much to bear, and that fracture allowed all the grief and panic that had been brimming over to bleed out of him. At that instant, those debilitating feelings didn't function anymore. Joey found he somehow had focus and could move.

The beast-man made a growling noise and lurched forward on his good leg, stalking ahead with his bad one lagging behind like a wounded comrade.

Joey took a step back.

Paul's killer took another stride forward.

Joey recognized the lake they had stumbled upon in the dead of night. He knew the Gauntlet lead around its bank and continued on the opposite side.

"Run, Clarence," Joey said to his friend, who stood with a wilted expression on the far side of the killer. "Run like hell. He can't chase us both."

Joey turned and charged down the trail.

The killer, caked in mud like some clay golem, followed right behind him.

As Joey ran, with his heart racing and sweat streaming down his face, he said a prayer just like he'd seen his Dad do. He asked God to help him out just one more time. He asked God to help him help himself.

The trail soon led to a hickory tree. This particular hickory had two knots above a gaping cavity in its trunk—the open mouth of an ancient wise-man sharing secrets with the brave souls who would journey long miles to seek his counsel.

The killer closed in behind him but moved much slower than Joey, who plunged his arm into the tree and snatched away leaves and twigs. He pulled out a dirty grocery bag and ripped open the plastic.

When he turned back to face the beast-man, Joey held a .45 caliber Smith & Wesson.

The killer stopped advancing fifty feet from Joey. He stood stone-cold still, and Joey knew those unseen eyes must have spotted the gun.

For a brief moment, Joey wondered if the man might retreat, walk right back in the direction he had come rather than face a bullet.

Then the killer resumed his advance, one labored step at a time. His stench clouded the air.

Joey recognized the weariness in the man. He saw the toll of old age, the way the killer hunkered and staggered, huffing and shuddering. The man's head hung low and bullish between his shoulders, glaring up through a curtain of hair and filth like something extinct and obsolete. The way he dragged his bad leg—this tree was falling.

Despite all Joey had endured, he was still standing. This was a new morning, and he had the blessing of youth. He had fresh blood and growing muscles and a reserve tank of energy. More than that, he had magic on his side—a blind faith in Jesus and Heaven and eternal life. He held fast to impossible dreams and had four friendly ghosts on his team who would never let him down. Only a kid could draw on that power, could use the Force or wield the hammer of Thor. Only a boy, not some old codger, could channel the sorcery of wizards and warlocks and harness the strength of dragonfire.

Joey knew the man before him was an agent of chaos, a murderous henchman of Satan, if not the Devil himself. This meant Joey had God in his corner, and God had given him the gift of a .45 caliber.

Joey steadied his phaser. He activated its photon charger and aimed at the great evil before him, dead-center mass, just like his dad had taught him.

From the sack on his back, the beast-man withdrew the enormous blade, the four-foot cleaver with two dorsal handles. The sack slid off his shoulder onto the ground. He tightened his fists on the weapon and squared his hulking frame at Joey. With a snarl and a deep roar, the man raised the cleaver and charged.

Picture yourself getting it right, then just act out the picture, Paul's voice echoed.

Joey fired. The gun's kick rocked him back.

The man seized with a jolt, but he did not fall.

Having courage doesn't mean you're never afraid, said his dad. *You overcome it.*

The killer lumbered ahead.

Joey steadied himself and fired again.

The man flinched at the shoulder. Then he took another stride toward him.

Aligning the gunsight with the killer's head, Joey searched for the eyes, looking for those black wormy tendrils spilling out of the sockets from all the evil within. All he saw was a tall, hairy man, ancient, slow, and wounded.

Joey shot, and a chunky mist burst from the back of that filthy head of hair.

The killer always *comes back,* Trainwreck reminded him. *You got to make sure it's final.*

With another blast, the killer's body tilted backward. In a fever, Joey squeezed the trigger again. Then again. The man was dead, but Joey—superhuman—marched ahead and fired a million more bullets from the magic gun of God, because *you got to make sure they can't come back for the sequel.* He kept squeezing that trigger to the sound of thunder until a friendly hand finally gripped his shoulder many ages later, and he fell into the arms of his fellow Bobcat, Clarence.

Joey and Clarence eventually made it home. The details and sequence of events were hazy for Joey, but he recalled that at some point on their hike out of the woods, Clarence regained cell reception and phoned his mother, who in turn called the authorities. By the time they made it back to Shady Grove Road, an armada of police cars had converged on the trailhead.

Mrs. Barkley was hysterical.

Joey's mother broke through a throng of officers and raced to him with a look of horror and relief. When she threw her arms around him, Joey wanted to never let go, especially once he saw Paul's mom and Davey's mom, leaning against a police car and holding each other.

Pandemonium followed.

The locals gathered hunting dogs and organized search parties. Something big had happened in a place where nothing much ever happened. Only urban legends and campfire tales.

Over the next two weeks, Joey spoke to dozens of police officers and avoided twice as many journalists. Trapper Valley had been overtaken by out-of-towners who showed up to report on multiple murders, organized crime, child heroes, monster sightings, mysterious killers, missing persons, and rumors of supernatural curses. Curiosity seekers arrived in droves to make YouTube videos and record live podcasts from Trapper Valley, Alabama, "cursed home of death and demon." Joey's mom's phone would not stop ringing, and for once, he was glad she had so far refused to buy him his own.

What Joey did recall were the funerals. He attended three

and found each of them crushing. Trainwreck's funeral proved the easiest to endure. His grandparents remained stoic, so everyone else tried to do the same. It's what Trainwreck would have wanted; no crybabies. At Davey's funeral, Joey felt awful seeing his little sister Ana kneeling at the side of his coffin while bawling her eyes out. And when he watched Candace Worton collapse to her knees crying in the aisle of the First Baptist Church, he wanted to tear the world apart.

#

In the end, it was the paper plane that won Tony Bianchi the scoop.

Joey had been taking out the trash, attempting to ignore the media people who loitered at the curb and snapped his photo. As he hauled the bulging black sack down the front steps to the garbage bin, an expertly folded aircraft—a jet fighter—glided across the breeze and landed squarely atop his load, right beneath his chin. He could not help but admire its workmanship and notice the handwriting on the wings.

He took it in hand before cramming the trash into the loaded bin, then unfolded it to read the message.

Dear Joey,

I'm Tony Bianchi with the Trapper Valley Gazette. We're the LOCAL paper! I know you're avoiding everybody else who's hounding you for your story, but I was hoping since I'm from around these parts, you'd make an exception in my case. I'd love to interview you, with your parents' consent and according to your terms. Give me a call if interested. Maybe if you tell your story, all these other pests will go

#

Tony Bianchi looked barely out of high school. Thin and fit in a blue Polo shirt and black eyeglasses, he had a wry smile and a gleam of wonder in his eyes. This made him seem more like a Bobcat and less like the vultures who'd been circling Joey's home for a headline.

"I want to thank all four of you for meeting with me," Tony said to Joey, Clarence, and their mothers from across a concrete picnic table Friday afternoon at Black Creek Park. "You had your choice of much bigger newspapers. I'm humbled you all chose me to tell your story."

Mrs. Kilgore raised her palms. "I'm only here to chaperone," she said softly. "This is Joey and Clarence's story."

Clarence sighed. "I'm just ready to put it all behind us."

His mother gave him a squeeze around the waist.

Joey gave the reporter a nod. "Your airplane worked."

Tony grinned. "I thought it might. In fact, from everything I've gathered about what happened…you guys remind me of my old friends and what it was like to grow up around here. All the fantastic stories we were told. And now you've actually lived one. Wow, what a story you lived…"

Joey felt as if he should reply but didn't know what to say.

Tony placed his phone on the table and pressed a red button icon to begin voice-recording. "I'm here to get the story from the source. I don't want to waste your time, so I'll jump right in.

"From what I understand, you guys survived quite the ordeal a few weeks ago on Black Oak Mountain, after a chance encounter with a couple of professional killers. Do I have that right?"

Joey and Clarence looked at each other. At first neither spoke, then Joey began, "We saw two men dumping bodies. I guess they were hiding the Goldstein family."

"That's right, the Goldsteins," Tony said, "the family of three from Hillbrook Heights. A real tragedy what happened there. So, you witnessed two people hiding bodies in the woods, and those people then wanted to eliminate the witnesses— meaning eliminate *you*. Is that correct?"

"That seemed to be the case," Joey said.

Tony looked at Clarence, who nodded but said nothing.

"That's when they came after us," Joey said. "Only me and Clarence survived."

"That is incredible. I'm so sorry you had to go through that. And you not only survived, but you brought down one of the killers." Tony said with a note of genuine awe. "Actually, *that's* what is incredible! You guys are bona fide heroes!"

"Our friends are named Paul Drabowksi and Davey Hopewell and Zack Traweek, but we always called Zack 'Trainwreck.'" Joey spelled each name, letter for letter, for the voice recorder. "Make sure to print those names in your story, because they're the real heroes. I don't feel much like a hero."

"Would you gentlemen care to talk about the final confrontation with the unidentified man in the woods? How did you feel at that moment? What was going through your mind?"

Joey and Clarence shared another look. A long one.

That fateful morning all rushed back in an instant…

Deep inside the forest, Joey staggered backward as the great gray giant lumbered toward him, stinking of rot. The beast-man bared his black teeth and raised up a blade the size of a railroad tie. Joey's breath seized in his chest, and he steadied the pistol to aim. The killer charged him…

Back in the park, Joey had his eyes squinted and his jaw clenched. He found himself frozen. Then he took a deep breath and forced the thoughts away.

"I don't remember too much," he said, eyes locked on the table top. "I might have blacked out. To tell the truth, I think it's best that way. I don't want to remember."

His mom rubbed the back of his neck.

Clarence shook his head and muttered, "That's not something I can really talk about. I don't even want to think about it. Mom told me the woods were cursed. I should've listened."

Clarence's mom gave a curt smile and knuckled his scalp playfully.

"According to police, they never found a second gunman," said Tony

"I guess not," Joey answered.

"But they discovered the remains of dozens of people inside the cave where the bodies were hidden. *Dozens!*" Tony stressed with a high pitch of excitement. "You guys were instrumental in not only solving the murder of a local family, but in uncovering a criminal conspiracy the details and implications of which are still largely unknown!"

Joey shrugged. "I don't know anything about that stuff."

"And from what's been reported, many of those bodies have been partially *devoured*," Tony emphasized the last word with a note of giddy intrigue. "What do you think could have done that?"

"The police suspect a bear," Clarence said.

"A bear with a taste for human blood," Tony said. "See any signs of a bear on the mountain?"

"Not exactly," Joey said. "But we saw worse, and they killed our friends."

Tony leaned back and bit his lip. "I am truly so sorry."

Joey felt his nose tickle and his vision blur but held back the tears with an iron will.

"Your group of friends…" Tony continued. "It was a Boy Scout troop, right?"

"No. Much cooler than that," Joey managed after clearing his throat. "We invented the club ourselves. We're called the Bobcats."

"Or…we *were* the Bobcats," Clarence added.

"*Were*?" Tony sounded concerned.

Joey saw the hurt on Clarence's face. He felt the same inside.

"We're the only members left," Clarence said. "It's tough to have a proper troop with just two Bobcats."

"I don't see how we could ever replace our friends," Joey said. "We used to meet in the equipment hut at the Trapper Valley Ballpark. Clarence and I decided we're gonna clean out the place Tuesday night. Call it quits."

Tony tilted his head and frowned. "I hate to hear that. I understand the sentiment, but wow, I've got to tell you…after following this story for the past few weeks, I am sincerely impressed with both of your grit and determination. The way you two hauled your injured buddy across the mountain during a thunderstorm… Sounds to me like the Bobcats were forging an extraordinary group of young men. It'd be a shame for it to come to an end."

Tony had more questions, and Clarence and Joey tried to answer them, but Joey's mind began to wander. He pondered the phrase *"extraordinary group of young men,"* and he did not remember how he responded.

#

The story hit the front page of the *Trapper Valley Gazette's* Sunday edition. The lead photo showed Joey and Clarence with arms around each other's shoulders. The headline stated simply, "Local Boys Become Heroes." Every store in town sold out.

#

Joey hadn't felt right since his return from the mountain, always restless, twitchy, itchy, and generally uncomfortable. His clothes no longer seemed to fit, and the room never kept the right temperature. Some indistinct agitation at the base of his brain would prickle and prod, making it impossible for him to relax or drop his guard. He could barely sleep, and nothing seemed to help. This made him feel particularly frazzled on his first Monday back to school, where he avoided the many stares and pretended not to hear the whispers.

At the moment, his mouth was dry. Unreasonably dry.

Parched. Finally, his turn arrived at the water fountain in the school hallway.

Joey stepped up and thumbed the switch. A silvery stream sprung forth in an arch.

"Hey, Kilgore," spoke a familiar voice from behind him.

Joey recognized the gravelly tones of Scotty Heckler. He turned around to face him, and as he did, cocked back his arm and balled his fist, reminding himself to lead with the middle knuckle.

Within a split second of losing his teeth, Scotty went, "No, no, no, no! You got it all wrong, man, I swear!"

The taller kid reeled back, and although Scotty had much bigger biceps, Joey saw fear in his eyes. This meant Scotty saw something altogether different in Joey—who stalled his punch and took a breath.

Scotty regained his footing while fanning the air with both hands as if trying to calm a large dog. "Look, I'm *sorry*. I mean it. That's all I wanted to say. I know I've been a real dick to you in the past, but I read what happened to you and your friends, and I'm sorry. Seriously. Sorry about everything."

A hush had fallen over the kids in the hall, who had all stopped to watch.

Joey realized his fist was still balled and his chest was rising up and down. He dropped his arm, flexed his fingers, then walked on down the hallway without a word.

#

The night was cool and quiet.

After their mothers had dropped them at the ballpark Tuesday evening at seven, Joey and Clarence convened at the equipment hut for their last official Bobcat meeting. Inside, they took down the various maps and posters from the cinderblock walls. They gathered their first-aid gear, their horseshoe set, and the cornhole game. They worked in almost total silence, and Joey figured it was not because they had nothing to say, but because they had far too much to say, so why bother.

In a shallow plastic bin, they collected spare tent stakes, a flint and steel set, two rolls of twine, and a rusty pocketknife. In the middle of this bin, Davey Hopewell's black-ink sketch of a ferocious bobcat snarled on the cover his ever-evolving official handbook, which lay there like some museum centerpiece to be protected but forgotten.

The work felt grim, but just as the sun was setting, a window brightened. Headlights shone through the glass then dimmed as a vehicle turned to park in the lot outside. A second flash meant another car was approaching.

Joey turned to Clarence, who looked curious and shrugged. Both of them went to the door and opened it to find people coming toward them down the walkway, and behind those people, a growing number of cars. These folks were filing straight for their meeting place and included several familiar faces.

Almost two dozen kids of different colors, classes, shapes and sizes arrived with their parents. Joey could hardly believe it. He saw his good friend Mitch from the old neighborhood. He saw Laney and Smitty, his two buds who'd been trying to organize a rugby team. His friend Leo from church came with his mom, and the Frazier brothers came with their dad. Joey had known those fellas for so long that he couldn't actually remember meeting them.

The first to walk up was a stranger—a slender girl with long red hair brushed behind her ears. She had sparkling green eyes and freckles across the bridge of her nose. She flashed a grin with a mischievous curve at one corner, which Joey found a little intimidating.

"I'm Jen," she said. "I'd like to be a Bobcat."

Joey didn't know what to say. He stood there dumbstruck as a line formed behind her. They must have all read the *Gazette*.

He began, "But we're shutting the—"

Clarence nudged an elbow into his ribs. "Joey? We have any rules against girls joining the troop?"

Joey searched and found his voice, although it cracked when he used it. "I don't think so."

Clarence beamed. He extended a hand to Jen. "Then, it's settled. I think I can speak for both of us when I say, welcome to the Bobcats!"

She took Clarence's hand and gave it two firm pumps up and down. He looked at Joey and winked. She would have to be taught the official handshake.

Joey's heart swelled. He felt sure that Trainwreck, Davey, and Paul were all watching this happen together somewhere, smiling down on him and Clarence from a better place and raising their thumbs high in approval of tonight's arrivals. Prospective Bobcats. New recruits. The future looked more promising than it had in a very long while.

"I guess the times are changing," Joey said.

Clarence clapped him on the shoulder and squeezed. "Get ready, buddy. Bobcats forever."

His friend's grip felt much like his father's had, and that was a wonderful thing.

Joey smiled. "Bobcats forever."

Acknowledgments

Thanks to my beautiful wife Shanna and my wonderful family for their unwavering support of my fictional pursuits. Thanks to my fellow rock-and-rollers in Skeptic? for being the baddest band in the whole damn 'Ham! Thanks to Chad Lutzke for his editorial feedback and for being a cool dude. Thanks to Jared Vickery for being Vic Kerry, and thanks to Robert McCammon for being Robert McCammon. If I were to thank all my old friends who shaped my childhood, shaped my adulthood, and shaped this book, I'd never finish these acknowledgments. I love all of you and I'll never forget you. Bobcats forever!

About the Author

Matthew Weber is editor and publisher of the *Double Barrel Horror* anthology series, the author of three short story collections (*A Dark & Winding Road*, *Seven Feet Under* and *Teeth Marks)* and the novel *The Bull*. He makes his living as editor of *Home Improvement and Repair* magazine (www.hirpub.com) and he plays bass in the long-running punk rock band Skeptic? He lives near Birmingham, Alabama, with his beautiful wife Shanna and his three awesome kids, Hudson, Miller and Maribeth. Find him online at www.pintbottlepress.com.

DOUBLE BARREL HORROR VOL. 3
STARRING:
CHRISTINE MORGAN
MARK MATTHEWS
GLENN ROLFE
THERESA BRAUN
CALVIN DEMMER
AND ROBERT ESSIG
6 AUTHORS, 12 CHILLING STORIES
EDITED BY MATTHEW WEBER

COLLECT ALL THREE!

DOUBLE BARREL HORROR VOL. 1
6 AUTHORS, 12 CHILLING STORIES
STARRING:
AMANDA HARD
K. TRAP JONES
VIC KERRY
J.C. MICHAEL
THE SISTERS OF SLAUGHTER
MATTHEW WEBER

DOUBLE BARREL HORROR VOL. 2
12 STORIES, 6 AUTHORS
STARRING
JOHN BODEN - SIMON DEWAR - PATRICK FREIVALD
CHAD LUTZKE - KAREN RUNGE - M.B. VUJACIC